THIS PROSPECTUS of the Flamingo list for 1996 is published in memory of Jonathan Warner, who was head of the imprint from October 1989 until his death in May 1994. It contains extracts from new works by many of the writers he brought to Flamingo, by some who were here when he arrived, and by others who we hope he would be glad to see have arrived since.

Jonathan's aim was to make Flamingo the most interesting and best-published list of literary writing in the UK, and to bring to it the most exciting new writers. His extraordinary success, in a relatively short time, is demonstrated by what is here.

He cared passionately about editing, that his writers' books should be as good as they could possibly be: a number of his authors have written about what an invigorating process this could be. He cared equally that they should be read, and those of us who worked with him knew what vigorous forms that determination took. We hope that he would have approved of this method of taking his writers to as many of their readers as we can find.

Stuart Proffitt
PUBLISHER
HARPERCOLLINS TRADE PUBLISHING

FLAMINGO
NEW FICTION

extracts from forthcoming titles

FEBRUARY – JULY 1996

Flamingo
An Imprint of HarperCollins*Publishers*

Flamingo
An Imprint of HarperCollins *Publishers*
77–85 Fulham Palace Road,
Hammersmith, London W6 8JB

Published by Flamingo 1996
1 3 5 7 9 8 6 4 2

ISBN 0 00 655003 7

Set in Linotron Galliard by
Rowland Phototypesetting Ltd,
Bury St Edmunds, Suffolk

Printed in Great Britain by
Caledonian International Book Manufacturing Ltd, Glasgow

Contents

AMY TAN

The Hundred Secret Senses

Olivia Yee is only five years old when Kwan, her seventeen-year-old half-sister from China, comes to live with the family and turns her world upside down. She is bombarded day and night with Kwan's stories from the world of Yin – romantic tales of ghosts who were once bandit maidens, strange accounts of missionaries and mercenaries from another world. Olivia just wants to lead a normal American life.

For the next thirty years, Olivia unhappily endures visits from Kwan and her ghosts, who appear in the living world to offer advice on everything from restaurants to Olivia's failed marriage. But just when Olivia cannot bear it any more, the revelations of a tragic, hundred-year-old family secret give her the opportunity to reconcile these ghosts from the past with the dreams of her future . . .

Both Amy Tan's novels, *The Joy Luck Club* and *The Kitchen God's Wife*, have become major international bestsellers. She lives in San Francisco.

FEBRUARY   £15.99   HARDBACK

The Hundred Secret Senses

I WAS NEARLY SIX by the time Kwan came to this country. We were waiting for her at the customs area of San Francisco Airport. Aunt Betty was also there. My mother was nervous and excited, talking nonstop: 'Now listen, kids, she'll probably be shy, so don't jump all over her . . . And she'll be skinny as a beanpole, so I don't want any of you making fun of her . . .'

When the customs official finally escorted Kwan into the lobby where we were waiting, Aunt Betty pointed and said, 'That's her. I'm telling you that's her.' Mom was shaking her head. This person looked like a strange old lady, short and chubby, not exactly the starving waif Mom pictured or the glamorous teenage sister I had in mind. She was dressed in drab gray pajamas, and her broad brown face was flanked by two thick braids.

Kwan was anything but shy. She dropped her bag, fluttered her arms, and bellowed, 'Hall-oo! Hall-oo!' Still hooting and laughing, she jumped and squealed the way our new dog did whenever we let him out of the garage. This total stranger tumbled into Mom's arms, then Daddy Bob's. She grabbed Kevin and Tommy by the shoulders and shook them. When she saw me, she grew quiet, squatted on the lobby floor, and held out her arms. I tugged on my mother's skirt. 'Is *that* my big sister?'

Mom said, 'See, she has your father's same thick, black hair.'

I still have the picture Aunt Betty took: curly-haired Mom in a mohair suit, flashing a quirky smile; our Italo-American stepfather, Bob, appearing stunned; Kevin and Tommy mugging in cowboy hats; a grinning Kwan with her hand on my shoulder; and me in a frothy party dress, my finger stuck in my bawling mouth.

I was crying because just moments before the photo was taken, Kwan had given me a present. It was a small cage of woven straw, which she pulled out of the wide sleeve of her coat and handed to me proudly. When I held it up to my eyes and peered between the webbing, I saw a six-legged monster, fresh-grass green, with saw-blade jaws, bulging eyes, and whips for eyebrows. I screamed and flung the cage away.

At home, in the bedroom we shared from then on, Kwan hung the cage with the grasshopper, now missing one leg. As soon as night fell, the grasshopper began to chirp as loudly as a bicycle bell warning people to get out of the way.

After that day, my life was never the same. To Mom, Kwan was a handy baby-sitter, willing, able, and free. Before my mother took off for an afternoon at the beauty parlor or shopping trip with her gal pals, she'd tell me to stick to Kwan. 'Be a good little sister and explain to her anything she doesn't understand. Promise?' So every day after school, Kwan would latch on to me and tag along wherever I went. By the first grade, I became an expert on public humiliation and shame. Kwan asked so many dumb questions that all the neighborhood kids thought she had come from Mars. She'd say: 'What M&M?' 'What ching gum?' 'Who this Popeye Sailor Man? Why one eye gone? He bandit?' Even Kevin and Tommy laughed.

With Kwan around, my mother could float guiltlessly through her honeymoon phase with Bob. When my teacher called Mom to say I was running a fever, it was Kwan who showed up at the nurse's office to take me home. When I fell while roller-skating, Kwan bandaged my elbows. She braided my hair. She packed lunches for Kevin, Tommy, and me. She tried to teach me to sing Chinese nursery songs. She soothed me when I lost a tooth. She ran the washcloth over my back while I took my bath.

I should have been grateful to Kwan. I could always depend on her. She liked nothing better than to be by my side. But instead, most of the time, I resented her for taking my mother's place.

I remember the day it first occurred to me to get rid of Kwan.

It was summer, a few months after she had arrived. Kwan, Kevin, Tommy, and I were sitting on our front lawn, waiting for something to happen. A couple of Kevin's friends sneaked to the side of our house and turned on the sprinkler system. My brothers and I heard the telltale spit and gurgle of water running into the lines, and we ran off just before a dozen sprinkler heads burst into spray. Kwan, however, simply stood there, getting soaked, marveling that so many springs had erupted out of the earth all at once. Kevin and his friends were howling with laughter. I shouted, 'That's not nice.'

Then one of Kevin's friends, a swaggering second-grader whom all the little girls had a crush on, said back to me, 'Is that dumb Chink your sister? Hey, Olivia, does that mean you're a dumb Chink too?'

I was so flustered I shouted, 'She's not my sister! I hate her! I wish she'd go back to China!' Tommy later told Daddy Bob what I had said, and Daddy Bob said, 'Louise, you better do something about your daughter.' My mother shook her head, looking sad. 'Olivia,' she said, 'we don't ever hate anyone. "Hate" is a *terrible* word. It hurts you as much as it hurts others.' Of course, this only made me hate Kwan even more.

The worst part was sharing my bedroom with her. At night, she liked to throw open the curtains so that the glare of the street lamp poured into our room, where we lay side by side in our matching twin beds. Under this 'beautiful American moon,' as she called it, Kwan would jabber away in Chinese. She kept on talking while I pretended to be asleep. She'd still be yakking when I woke up. That's how I became the only one in our family who learned Chinese. Kwan infected me with it. I absorbed her language through my pores while I was sleeping. She pushed her Chinese secrets into my brain and changed how I thought about the world. Soon I was even having nightmares in Chinese.

In exchange, Kwan learned her English from me – which, now that I think of it, may be the reason she has never spoken it all that well. I was not an enthusiastic teacher. One time, when I was seven, I played a mean trick on her. We were lying in our beds in the dark.

'Libby-ah,' Kwan said. And then she asked in Chinese, 'The delicious pear we ate this evening, what's its American name?'

'Barf,' I said, then covered my mouth to keep her from hearing my snickers.

She stumbled over this new sound – 'bar-a-fa, bar-a-fa' – before she said, 'Wah! What a clumsy word for such a delicate taste. I never ate such good fruit. Libby-ah, you are a lucky girl. If only my mother did not die.' She could segue from just about any topic to the tragedies of her former life, all of which she conveyed to me in our secret language of Chinese.

Another time, she watched me sort through Valentine's Day cards I had spilled on to my bed. She came over and picked up a card. 'What's this shape?'

'It's a heart. It means love. See, all the cards have them. I have to give one to each kid in my class. But it doesn't really mean I love everyone.'

She went back to her own bed and lay down. 'Libby-ah,' she said. 'If only my mother didn't die of heartsickness.' I sighed, but didn't look at her. This again. She was quiet for a few moments, then went on. 'Do you know what heartsickness is?'

'What?'

'It's warming your body next to your family, then having the straw roof blow off and carry you away.'

'Oh.'

'You see, she didn't die of lung sickness, no such thing.'

And then Kwan told me how our father caught a disease of too many good dreams. He could not stop thinking about riches and an easier life, so he became lost, floated out of their lives, and washed away his memories of the wife and baby he left behind.

'I'm not saying our father was a bad man,' Kwan whispered hoarsely. 'Not so. But his loyalty was not strong. Libby-ah, do you know what loyalty is?'

'What?'

'It's like this. If you ask someone to cut off his hand to save you from flying off with the roof, he immediately cuts off both hands to show he is more than glad to do so.'

'Oh.'

'But our father didn't do this. He left us when my mother was about to have another baby. I'm not telling you lies, Libby-ah, this is true. When this happened, I was four years old by my Chinese age. I can never forget lying against my mother, rubbing her swollen belly. Like a watermelon, she was this big.'

She reached out her arms as far as she could. 'Then all the water in her belly poured out as tears from her eyes, she was so sad.' Kwan's arms fell suddenly to her sides. 'That poor starving baby in her belly ate a hole in my mother's heart, and they both died.'

I'm sure Kwan meant some of this figuratively. But as a child, I saw everything Kwan talked about as literal truth: chopped-off hands flying out of a roofless house, my father floating on the China Sea, the little baby sucking on his mother's heart. The images became phantoms. I was like a kid watching a horror movie, with my hands clapped to my eyes, peering anxiously through the cracks. I was Kwan's willing captive, and she was my protector.

At the end of her stories, Kwan would always say: 'You're the only one who knows. Don't tell anyone. Never. Promise, Libby-ah?'

And I would always shake my head, then nod, drawn to allegiance through both privilege and fear.

One night, when my eyelids were already heavy with sleep, she started droning again in Chinese: 'Libby-ah, I must tell you something, a forbidden secret. It's too much of a burden to keep inside me any longer.'

I yawned, hoping she'd take the hint.

'I have yin eyes.'

'What eyes?'

'It's true. I have yin eyes. I can see yin people.'

'What do you mean?'

'Okay, I'll tell you. But first you must promise never to tell anyone. Never. Promise, ah?'

'Okay. Promise.'

'Yin people, they are those who have already died.'

My eyes popped open. 'You see dead people? . . . You mean, *ghosts?*'

'Don't tell anyone. Never. Promise, Libby-ah?'

I stopped breathing. 'Are there ghosts here now?' I whispered.

'Oh yes, many. Many, many good friends.'

I threw the covers over my head. 'Tell them to go away,' I pleaded.

'Don't be afraid. Libby-ah, come out. They're your friends too. Oh see, now they're laughing at you for being so scared.'

I began to cry. After a while, Kwan sighed and said in a disappointed voice. 'All right, don't cry anymore. They're gone.'

So that's how the business of ghosts got started. When I finally came out from under the covers, I saw Kwan sitting straight up, illuminated by the artificial glow of her American moon, staring out the window as if watching her visitors recede into the night.

The next morning, I went to my mother and did what I promised I'd never do: I told her about Kwan's yin eyes.

Kwan's now nearly fifty, whereas I'm a whole twelve years younger, a point she proudly mentions whenever anyone politely asks which of us is older. In front of other people, she likes to pinch my cheek and remind me that my skin is getting 'wrinkle up' because I smoke cigarettes and drink too much wine and coffee – bad habits she does not have. 'Don't hook on, don't need stop,' she's fond of saying. Kwan is neither deep nor subtle; everything's right on the surface, for anybody to see. The point is, no one would ever guess we are sisters.

Kevin once joked that maybe the Communists sent us the wrong kid, figuring we Americans thought all Chinese people looked alike anyway. After hearing that, I fantasized that one day we'd get a letter from China saying, 'Sorry, folks. We made a mistake.'

In so many ways, Kwan never fit into our family. Our annual Christmas photo looked like those children's puzzles, 'What's Wrong with This Picture?' Each year, front and center, there was Kwan – wearing brightly colored summer clothes, plastic bow-tie barrettes on both sides of her head, and a loony grin big enough to burst her cheeks. Eventually, Mom found her a job as a busgirl at a Chinese-American restaurant. It took Kwan a month to realize the food they served there was supposed to be Chinese. Time did nothing to either Americanize her or bring out her resemblance to our father.

On the other hand, people tell me I'm the one who takes after him most, in both appearance and personality. 'Look how much Olivia can eat without gaining an ounce,' Aunt Betty is forever saying. 'Just like Jack.' My mother once said, 'Olivia analyzes every single detail to death. She has her father's accountant mentality. No wonder she became a photographer.' Those kinds of comments make me wonder what else had been passed along to me through my father's genes. Did I inherit from him my dark moods, my fondness for putting salt on my fruit, my phobia about germs?

Kwan, in contrast, is a tiny dynamo, barely five feet tall, a miniature bull in a china shop. Everything about her is loud and clashing. She'll wear a purple checked jacket over turquoise pants. She whispers loudly in a husky voice, sounding as if she had chronic laryngitis, when in fact she's never sick. She dispenses health warnings, herbal recommendations, and opinions on how to fix just about anything, from broken cups to broken marriages. She bounces from topic to topic, interspersing tips on where to find bargains. Tommy once said that Kwan believes in free speech, free association, free car-wash with fill-'er-up. The only change in Kwan's English over the last thirty years is the speed with which she talks. Meanwhile, she thinks her English is great. She often corrects her husband. 'Not *stealed*,' she'll tell George. '*Stolened*.'

In spite of all our obvious differences, Kwan thinks she and I are exactly alike. As she sees it, we're connected by a cosmic

Chinese umbilical cord that's given us the same inborn traits, personal motives, fate, and luck. 'Me and Libby-ah,' she tells new acquaintances, 'we same in here.' And she'll tap the side of my head. 'Both born Year the Monkey. Which one older? You guess. Which one?' And then she'll squash her cheek against mine.

Kwan has never been able to correctly pronounce my name, Olivia. To her, I will always be Libby-ah, not plain Libby, like the tomato juice, but Libby-ah, like the nation of Muammar Qaddafi. As a consequence, her husband, George Lew, his two sons from a first marriage, and that whole side of the family all call me Libby-ah too. The 'ah' part especially annoys me. It's the Chinese equivalent of saying 'hey,' as in 'Hey, Libby, come here.' I asked Kwan once how she'd like it if I introduced her to everyone as 'Hey, Kwan.' She slapped my arm, went breathless with laughter, then said hoarsely, 'I like, I like.' So much for cultural parallels, Libby-ah it is, forever and ever.

I'm not saying I don't love Kwan. How can I not love my own sister? In many respects, she's been more like a mother to me than my real one. But I often feel bad that I don't want to be close to her. What I mean is, we're *close* in a manner of speaking. We know things about each other, mostly through history, from sharing the same closet, the same toothpaste, the same cereal every morning for twelve years, all the routines and habits of being in the same family. I really think Kwan is sweet, also loyal, extremely loyal. She'd tear off the ear of anyone who said an unkind word about me. That counts for a lot. It's just that I wouldn't want to be closer to her, not the way some sisters are who consider themselves best friends. As it is, I don't share everything with her the way she does with me, telling me the most private details of her life – like what she told me last week about her husband:

'Libby-ah,' she said, 'I found mole, big as my nostril, found on – what you call this thing between man legs, in Chinese we say *yinnang*, round and wrinkly like two walnut?'

'Scrotum.'

'Yes-yes, found big mole on scrotum! Now every day – every

day, must examine Georgie-ah, his scrotum, make sure this mole don't start grow.'

To Kwan, there are no boundaries among family. Everything is open for gruesome and exhaustive dissection – how much you spent on your vacation, what's wrong with your complexion, the reason you look as doomed as a fish in a restaurant tank. And then she wonders why I don't make her a regular part of my social life. She, on the other hand, invites me to dinner once a week, as well as to every boring family gathering – last week, a party for George's aunt, celebrating the fact that she received her U.S. citizenship after fifty years, that sort of thing. Kwan thinks only a major catastrophe would keep me away. She'll worry aloud: 'Why you don't come last night? Something the matter?'

'Nothing's the matter.'

'Feel sick?'

'No.'

'You want me to come over, bring you orange? I have extra, good price, six for one dollar.'

'Really, I'm *fine*.'

She's like an orphan cat, kneading on my heart. She's been this way all my life, peeling me oranges, buying me candy, admiring my report cards and telling me how smart I was, smarter than she could ever be. Yet I've done nothing to endear myself to her. As a child, I often refused to play with her. Over the years, I've yelled at her, told her she embarrassed me. I can't remember how many times I've lied to get out of seeing her.

Meanwhile, she has *always* interpreted my outbursts as helpful advice, my feeble excuses as good intentions, my pallid gestures of affection as loyal sisterhood. And when I can't bear it any longer, I lash out and tell her she's crazy. Before I can retract the sharp words, she pats my arm, smiles and laughs. And the wound she bears heals itself instantly. Whereas I feel guilty forever.

CHARLES D'AMBROSIO

The Point

Like the best stories of Raymond Carver, Charles D'Ambrosio's prize-winning fiction is full of light and humour even in its darkest visions. These are stories of people struggling to wrest meaning from the tragedies that hover over their lives. Richly textured and finely poised, these fictions reveal a landscape of arresting beauty and inevitable sorrow. They are packed with incident, bold in their narrative sweep and written with a distinctive grace and measured dignity which impresses itself from their very first lines. *The Point* marks the debut of an exceptionally fine new talent, as Charles D'Ambrosio takes his place among the most interesting and exciting American writers working today.

'A significant new American voice'   JAY MCINERNY

Charles D'Ambrosio's fiction has appeared in the *New Yorker*, *Paris Review*, *Best American Short Stories 1991* and *The Picador Book of American Short Stories*. He was the winner of the 1993 Aga Khan Prize for fiction.

MARCH   £9.99   HARDBACK

Her Real Name

THE GIRL'S SCALP looked as though it had been singed by fire – strands of thatchy red hair snaked away from her face, then settled against her skin, pasted there by sweat and sunscreen and the blown grit and dust of travel. For a while her thin hair had remained as light and clean as the down of a newborn chick, but it was getting hotter as they drove west, heading into a summer-long drought that scorched the landscape, that withered the grass and melted the black tar between expansion joints in the road and bloated like balloons the bodies of raccoon and deer and dog and made everything on the highway ahead ripple like a mirage through waves of rising heat. Since leaving Fargo, it had been too hot to wear the wig, and it now lay on the seat between them, still holding within its webbing the shape of her head. Next to it, a bag of orange candy – *smiles*, she called them – spilled across the vinyl. Sugar crystals ran into the dirty stitching and stuck to her thigh. Gum wrappers and greasy white bags littered the floor, and on the dash, amid a flotsam of plastic cups, pennies, and matchbooks, a bumper sticker curled in the heat. EXPECT A MIRACLE, it read.

The girl cradled a black Bible in her lap, the leather covers as worn and ragged as old tennis shoes. The inner leaf contained a family tree dating back to 1827, names tightly scrawled in black against yellow parchment, a genealogy as ponderous as those kept in Genesis, the book of the generations of Adam. The list of ancestors on the inner leaf was meaningless ancient history to the man, whose name was Jones, but the girl said her family had carried that same Bible with them wherever they went, for one

15

hundred and fifty years, and that she wanted it with her too. 'That's me,' the girl had said, showing Jones her name, the newest of all, penned in generous loops of Bic blue. She'd written it in herself along the margin of the page. *b. 1960–*. The girl read different passages aloud as they drove, invoking a mix of epic beauty and bad memories, of Exodus and the leather belt her stepfather used to beat her when she broke a commandment – one of the original ten or one of his additions. Jones wasn't sure what faith she placed in the austere Christianity of her forefathers, but reading aloud seemed to cast a spell over her. She had a beautiful church-trained voice that lifted each verse into a soothing melody, a song whose tune of succor rose and fell somewhere beyond the harsh demands of faith. Only minutes before she'd read herself to sleep with a passage from Jeremiah.

Now, as if she felt Jones staring, the girl stirred.

'You were looking at me,' she said. 'You were thinking something.'

Her face was shapeless, soft and pale as warm putty.

'I could feel it,' she said. 'Where are we?'

They hadn't gone more than a mile since she'd dozed off. She reached for the candy on the seat.

'You hungry? You want a smile, Jones?'

'No, none for me,' Jones said.

'A Life Saver?' She held the unraveled package out.

'Nothing, thanks.'

'Me eating candy, and my teeth falling out.' The girl licked the sugar off a smile and asked, 'How far to Las Vegas?'

Jones jammed a tape in the eight-track. He was driving a 1967 Belvedere he'd bought for seven hundred dollars cash in Newport News, and it had come with a bulky eight-track, like an atavistic organ, bolted beneath the glove box. He'd found two tapes in the trunk, and now, after fifteen thousand miles, he was fairly sick of both Tom Jones and Steppenwolf. But he preferred the low-fidelity noise of either tape to the sound of himself lying.

16

'Why don't you come with me, little girl,' he sang along, in a high, mocking falsetto, 'on a magic carpet ride.'

'How far?' the girl asked.

Jones adjusted his grip on the steering wheel. 'Another day, maybe.'

She seemed to fall asleep again, her dry-lidded eyes shut like a lizard's, her parched, flaking lips parted, her frail body given over to the car's gentle rocking. Jones turned his attention back to the road, a hypnotic black line snaking through waves of yellow grass. It seemed to Jones that they'd been traveling through eastern Montana forever, that the same two or three trees, the same two or three farmhouses and grain silos were rushing past like scenery in an old movie, only suggesting movement. Endless fields, afire in the bright sun, were occasionally broken by stands of dark cottonwood or the gutted chassis of a rusting car. Collapsing barns leaned over in the grass, giving in to the hot wind and the insistent flatness, as if passively accepting the laws of a world whose only landmark, as far as Jones could see, was the level horizon.

'He's out there,' the girl said. 'I can feel him out there when I close my eyes. He knows where we are.'

'I doubt that very much,' Jones said.

The girl struggled to turn, gripping the headrest. She looked through the rear window at the warp of the road as it narrowed to a pinprick on the pale edge of the world they'd left behind: it was out of the vanishing point that her father would come.

'I expect he'll be caught up soon,' she said. 'He's got a sense. One time he predicted an earthquake.'

'It's a big country,' Jones said. 'We could've gone a million other ways. Maybe if you think real hard about Florida that'll foul up his super-duper predicting equipment.'

'Prayer,' the girl said. 'He prays. Nothing fancy. We're like Jonah sneaking on that boat in Tarshish; they found him out.'

The girl closed her eyes; she splashed water on her face and chest.

'It's so hot,' she said. 'Tell me some more about the Eskimos.'

'I'm running out of things to say about Eskimos,' Jones said. 'I only read that one book.'

'Say old stuff, I don't care.'

He searched his memory for what he remembered of Knud Rasmussen.

'Nothing's wasted,' Jones said. 'They use everything. The Inuit can make a sled out of a slain dog. They kill the dog and skin it, then cut the hide into two strips.'

'I'm burning alive,' the girl said.

'They roll up the hide and freeze the strips in water to make the runners. Then they join the runners together with the dog's rib bones.' Jones nibbled the corner of an orange smile. 'One minute the dog's pulling the sled, the next minute he is the sled.' He saw that the girl was asleep. 'That's irony,' he said and then repeated the word. 'Irony.' It sounded weak, inadequate; it described nothing; he drove silently on. Out through the windshield he saw a landscape too wide for the eye to measure – the crushing breadth of the burnt fields and the thin black thread of road vanishing into a vast blue sky as if the clouds massed on the horizon were distant cities, and they were going to them.

She'd been working the pumps and the register at a crossroads station in southern Illinois, a rail-thin girl with stiff red hair the color of rust, worried, chipped nails, and green eyes without luster. She wore gray coveralls that ballooned over her body like a clown's outfit, the long legs and sleeves rolled into thick cuffs. 'I've never seen the ocean,' she'd said, pointing to the remains of a peeling bumper sticker on Jones's car . . . BE SAILING, it read. She stood on the pump island while Jones filled his tank. The hooded blue lights above them pulsed in sync to the hovering sound of cicadas, and both were a comforting close presence in the black land spreading out around the station. Jones wanted to tell the girl to look around her, right now: this flat patch of nothing was as good as an ocean. Instead, making conversation, Jones said, 'I just got out of the navy.'

'You from around here?' she asked.

'Nope,' Jones said.

He topped off his tank and reached into the car where he kept his money clipped to the sun visor.

'I knew that,' she said. 'I seen your plates.'

Jones handed her a twenty from his roll of muster pay. The money represented for him his final six months in the navy, half a year in which he hadn't once set foot on land. Tired of the sea, knowing he'd never make a career out of it, on his last tour Jones had refused the temptations of shore leave, hoping to hit land with enough of a stake to last him a year. Now, as he looked at the dwindling roll, he was torn between exhaustion and a renewed desire to move on before he went broke.

'Where in Virginia you from?'

'I'm not,' Jones said. 'I bought the car in Newport News. Those are just old plates.'

'That's too bad,' the girl said. 'I like the name. Virginia. Don't you?'

'I guess it's not special to me one way or the other,' Jones said.

The girl folded the twenty in half and ran her thin fingers back and forth over the crease. That she worked in a gas station in the middle of nowhere struck Jones as sexy, and now he looked at her closely, trying to decide whether or not he wanted to stop a night or two in Carbondale. Except for the strange texture and tint of her red hair, he thought she looked good, and the huge coveralls, rippling in the breeze, made her seem sweet and lost, somehow innocent and alone in a way that gave Jones the sudden confidence that he could pick her up without much trouble.

'You gonna break that?' Jones asked, nodding at the bill.

Her arm vanished entirely as she reached into the deep pocket of her coveralls and pulled out a roll of bills stained black with grease and oil. Jones took the change, then looked off, around the station. In the east a dome of light rose above Carbondale, a pale yellow pressing out against the night sky. The road running in front of the station was empty except for a spotlight that shone on a green dinosaur and a Sinclair sign that spun on a pole above it.

'Don't get scared, working out here?' he asked.

'Nah,' she said. 'Hardly anyone comes out this way, 'less they're like you, 'less they're going somewhere. Had a man from Vernal gas here the other night. That's in Utah.'

'Still –'

'Some nights I wouldn't care if I got robbed.'

Jones took his toilet kit – a plastic sack that contained a thin, curved bonelike bar of soap, a dull razor, and a balding toothbrush – out of the glove box. 'You mind if I wash up?'

'Washroom's around back,' she said. 'By the propane tanks.'

In the bathroom, he took off his T-shirt and washed himself with a wetted towel, watching his reflection in the mirror above the sink as though it were someone else, someone from his past. Gray eyes, a sharp sculpted jaw, ears that jutted absurdly from his close-cropped head: a navy face. Six months of shipboard isolation had left him with little sense of himself outside of his duties as an officer. In that time, held in the chrysalis of his berth, he'd forgotten not only what he looked like, but what other people might see when they looked at him. Now he was a civilian. He decided to shave, lathering up with the bar of soap. The mustache came off in four or five painful strokes.

For a moment the warm breeze was bracing against his cleanly shaven face. He stood in the lot, a little stiff, at attention, and when the girl waved to him from the cashier's window, Jones saluted.

'See you later,' he said.

'Okay,' she said.

Jones drove away, stopping at a convenience store about a mile down the road. He grabbed two six-packs, a cheap Styrofoam cooler, and a bag of ice and wandered down the aisle where the toys were kept. He selected a pink gun that fired rubber suction darts. He returned to the station and parked his car in the shadow of the dinosaur. He waited. The girl sat in the glass booth behind a rack of road atlases, suddenly the sweetheart of every town he'd traveled through in the last few months. To be with someone who knew his name, to hear another voice would be enough for tonight. Jones twisted open a beer and loaded the dart gun. He licked the suction tip, took aim and fired.

'Hey,' the girl shouted.

'Wanna go somewhere?' Jones asked.

They'd crossed the Mississippi three weeks ago and driven north through Iowa, staying in motels and eating in restaurants, enjoying high times until his money began to run out. Then they started sleeping in the car, parked at rest stops or in empty lots, arms and legs braided together in the backseat of the Belvedere. One morning Jones had gone to a bakeshop and bought a loaf of day-old sourdough bread for thirty-five cents. It was the cool blue hour before dawn, but already, as he crossed the parking lot, the sky was growing pale, and the patches of tar were softening beneath his shoes, and in the sultry air the last weak light of the street lamps threw off dull coronas of yellow and pink. Only one other car was parked in the empty lot, and its windows had been smashed out, a spray of glass scattered like seeds across the asphalt. As Jones approached the Belvedere, he saw the girl slowly lift the hair away from her head. It was as if he were witness to some miracle of revelation set in reverse, as if the rising sun and the new day had not bestowed but instead stripped the world of vision, exposed and left it bare. Her skull was blue, a hidden thing not meant for the light. Jones opened her door. She held the wig of curly red hair in her lap.

'Damn,' he said. He paced off a small circle in the parking lot.

The girl combed her fingers calmly through the hair on her lap. She'd understood when she removed the wig that revealing herself to Jones would tip fate irrevocably. She felt that in this moment she would know Jones and know him forever. She waited for Jones to spend his shock and anger, afraid that when he cooled down she might be on her way back to Carbondale, to the gas station

21

and her stepfather and the church and the prayers for miraculous intercession. When Jones asked what was wrong with her, and she told him, he punted the loaf of sourdough across the empty lot.

'Why haven't you said anything?'

'What was I supposed to say, Jones?'

'The truth might've made a good start.'

'Seems to me you've been having yourself a fine time without it,' she said. 'Hasn't been all that crucial so far.'

'Jesus Christ.'

'Besides, I wouldn't be here now if I'd told you. You'd have been long gone.'

Jones denied it. 'You don't know me from Adam,' he said.

'Maybe not,' she said. She set the wig on her head. 'I'll keep it on if you think I'm ugly.' The girl swung her legs out of the car and walked across the lot. She picked up the bread and brought it back. 'These things drag out,' she said.

She brushed pebbles and dirt and splinters of glass from the crust and then cracked the loaf in half.

'You didn't get any orange juice, did you?' she asked. 'This old bread needs orange juice.'

She reached inside and tore a hunk of clean white bread from the core and passed the loaf to Jones. He ate a piece and calmed down.

'Who knows how long I've got?' she said.

When they headed out again that morning, going west seemed inevitable – driving into the sun was too much to bear, and having it at their backs in the quiet and vacant dawn gave them the feeling, however brief, that they could outrace it. It was 1977, it was August, it was the season when the rolling fields were feverish with sunflowers turning on withered stalks to reach the light, facing them in the east as they drove off at dawn, gazing after them in the west as the sun set and they searched the highway ahead for the softly glowing neon strip, for the revolving signs and lighted windows and the melancholy trickle of small-town traffic that would bloom brightly on the horizon and mean food and a place to stop for the night. If Jones wasn't too tired, he pushed on, preferring the solitude of night driving, when actual distances collapsed unseen, and the car seemed to float unmoored through limitless space, the reassuring hum of tires rolling beneath him, the lights of town hovering across the darkened land like constellations in a warm universe. By day, he stopped only when the girl wanted to see a natural wonder, a landmark, a point of historical interest. Early this morning they'd visited the valley of the Little Bighorn. Silence held sway over the sight, a silence that touched the history of a century ago and then reached beyond it, running back to the burnt ridges and bluffs and to a time when the flat golden plain in the West had not yet felt the weight of footprints. Jones watched the girl search among the huddled white markers, looking for the blackened stone where Custer fell. She'd climbed over the wrought-iron fence to stand beside the stone, and a bull snake cooling in the shadow slithered off through the yellow grass. She seemed okay, not really sick, only a little odd and alien when she took off the wig. Now and then Jones would look at the girl and think, *You're dying*, but the unvarying heat hammered the days into a dull sameness, and driving induced a kind of amnesia, and for the most part Jones had shoved the idea out of his mind until this morning when they'd discussed their next move.

'We could drive to Nevada,' she'd said. 'Seems we're headed that direction, anyhow.'

'Maybe,' Jones said.

'It only takes an hour to get married,' the girl said, 'and they rent you the works. A veil, flowers. We'll gamble. I've never done that. Have you? Roulette – what do you think, Jones?'

'I said maybe.'

'Jones,' she said. 'I'm not into maybe.'

'I don't know,' Jones said. 'I haven't thought it out.'

'What's to think?' the girl said. 'You'd be a widower in no time.'

Jones squeezed the girl's knee, knobby and hard like a foal's. 'Jesus,' he said.

'It's not a big commitment I'm asking for.'

'Okay, all right,' Jones had said. 'Don't get morbid.'

SUE MILLER

The Distinguished Guest

At the age of seventy-two, Lily Roberts suddenly became a national celebrity by writing her first book, a spiritual memoir. But her new-found fame was not well received by her children. Her architect son, Alan, and daughter, Clary, were profoundly disturbed by Lily's intimate revelations about her married life. Ten years on, their resentment is still raw, and when Lily, now ill and frail, comes to live with Alan and his own family, the bitter legacy of their very differing memories threatens to upset the precarious balance of all their lives . . .

'Wonderful stuff – rich, intelligent and moving. This is the fiction we need.'   *Los Angeles Times*

Sue Miller is the acclaimed author of *Inventing the Abbotts*, *The Good Mother*, *Family Pictures* and *For Love*. She lives in Boston.

MARCH   £15.99   HARDBACK
£9.99   PAPERBACK

The Distinguished Guest

GABY PADDED BAREFOOT around the dark kitchen, her hands moving quickly and surely in and out among the familiar shadowy shapes, making coffee. Every time she opened the refrigerator, a knife of light slashed into the room and she had to squint her eyes shut, but she didn't turn the lights on. She never did. She didn't like to at this hour. *Her* hour, of the day. Of the night.

'How do you stand it?' her friends asked her. 'God, four A.M., I could never do it.' But this was Gaby's routine, she was used to it. Not just used to it – she'd chosen it, she'd shaped it. At work by four-thirty, she was usually home again around two. In mid-afternoon she napped for several hours and then, around five, she got up and returned once more to the shop for an hour or so to close up.

It had been the children who had waked her in the past, returning noisily from their after-school activities, banging the doors of whatever house they were in, thumping and clattering, dropping things – books, musical instruments, sports equipment. Now it was Alan, who came in and gently touched her shoulder. Often they sat and talked in a desultory intimacy as she came slowly awake. This had come to be, too, the time of day they were most likely to make love, with the late sun streaming in the room and lying with a warm, hard light across their aging bodies. And in the last few years, he'd taken to coming back to the shop with her almost every day and helping her with the closing up.

In the winter, yes, sometimes she did mind it. It was especially hard sliding into the frigid embrace of the car in the darkness, her

27

breath pluming smokily from her nose. The car's heater would just have begun to blow tepid air on her legs by the time she was pulling up at the shop. The shop itself was cold and hollow-feeling until the oven's heat and the odor of baking made the space seem slowly smaller and more welcoming.

She loved these days though, the pale darkness of summer. The windows were open to the noises of daybreak – the first delicate stirrings of trees in the wind, the fierce, awakened energy of the birds. And she loved to watch the pearly light imperceptibly arriving as she moved alone in her house while Alan still slept. Alan, and Lily today. She'd been there four days.

And had already seemingly made herself perfectly at home. They'd put her in the guest suite and arranged it as she requested, as a kind of bedroom-office. Lily had immediately settled into a routine centered on her work – boxes of papers she'd sent ahead by train and now had Alan set out around her worktable for her. And they had settled into a routine too, centered on her.

It was clear to Gaby that Alan was having more difficulty adjusting to Lily's presence than she was. And it was true that when she was with them, Lily *presided*, in a sense, in spite of having to make her pronouncements in a weakened, whispery voice. She could be biting, she could be sarcastic, and Alan often responded with his own version of the same thing.

Partly for this reason, Gaby has been getting the old woman ready for bed at night. Alan gets her to the bathroom in the morning and leaves her sitting in bed with coffee, awaiting Noreen, the woman they've hired to help out. Since Noreen leaves before dinner each day, Gaby decided quickly that it would be better for both Alan and Lily if she were the one with bedtime duty.

She has surprised herself with the tenderness she sometimes feels for Lily as she performs this service. Just last night, as Gaby was leading her from the bathroom to the bedroom to help her get undressed, Lily whispered in that rushed, breathless way, ' "When you shall be old, you shall stretch forth your hands and another shall gird thee and carry thee whither thou wouldst not go."'

'Ah,' Gaby had said, for want of anything better to say. Was this a protest?

'John. The Book of John,' Lily whispered.

'Oh yes!' Gaby said, as though she recollected the passage.

Lily sat carefully down on the edge of the bed. She tilted her head back and her face labored a moment. Then she incanted softly, ' "When you were young, you girded yourself and walked whither thou wouldst: but when thou shalt be old, thou shalt stretch forth thy hands and another shall gird thee and carry thee whither thou wouldst not."'

A few moments later, as Gaby knelt down to untie and remove Lily's shoes, she had a sense, suddenly, of doing something holy, something that made her feel, in some deep way, *of use*. Holding the shapeless foot in its thick stocking on her lap, she had felt tears of compassion and love spring to her eyes.

But then there are the other moments, those moments when Lily seems in one way or another to sneer at Alan. At these times Alan seems unable to resist carping back, and the two of them seem then to Gaby not so much like mother and son as like jealous siblings, each of them resentful of the very air the other takes in. It reminds her sometimes of the squabbles Ettie and Thomas got into when they were small; and her irritation now reminds her, too, of the rage she felt at her sons when they bickered and teased each other, when they wailed and called to her to adjudicate. Once, she remembers, wincing, she had banged their heads together to stop a fight; and then screamed at them in helpless, high-pitched French that they would drive her mad.

Of course, with Alan and Lily, Gaby isn't free to distribute her anger evenly, and so it's Alan she feels herself turning away from. Last night, he'd come out from their bedroom to find her skimming through the Bible. 'Jesus, Gaby, what are you *doing*?' he asked.

She'd been annoyed instantly, but she held her voice level.

'Looking for something your mother just said to me, about being led around by others when you're old.'

'It's in the Bible?' He sounded offended by this very idea.

'She said it was John. Do you know it?'

'I know nothing about the Bible. Nothing.' His voice was flat and absolute. She watched him. Lanky, barefoot, he crossed to the island, went behind it. She watched him open the refrigerator, stand in front of it for a moment, looking. He shut it without having taken anything out, and left the room. Of course he knew the Bible! Whole passages by heart. How absurd for him to deny this! Gaby had snapped the book closed.

She sat now at the wide kitchen island that separated the cooking and living areas of the house and lifted her oversized white coffee cup. In the dusky light, the room was beginning to take shape, the low sleek forms of the furniture Alan had chosen in their familiar places. Among them now loomed the humps and curves of Lily's furniture, five Victorian pieces come down from her family that she wanted Alan and Gaby to have. In this half-light, they made Gaby think of the hulking beasts, the imaginary monsters of childhood – *wild things* – and she smiled.

They'd arrived before Lily, sent ahead by train too, along with the dozen or so heavy cartons of books and papers. Alan had assumed that Lily would take the furniture with her when she left. Thomas had helped Alan, and they'd crammed everything into the guest room to make Lily feel at home. Gaby had directed the removal of a few of their own things, and the placement of Lily's possessions.

Lily had been astounded when she'd arrived. Didn't they realize her intentions? These chairs and tables were gifts! She'd kept what she wanted, she assured them. It was all in storage at the retirement community until she could move in. These were for Alan and Gaby, to do with as they wished. And she insisted that they be moved right back out into the living room.

Gaby took another swallow of coffee. Odd, she thought. It had taken Lily to add the element that made her feel at home in this house at last. When they'd moved in, they'd discarded most of their old furniture, things they'd acquired cheaply over the years at yard sales or flea markets, or as friends cast them away. Alan had a vision of how he wanted the house to look, and the old stuff didn't fit it. Besides, some of the new furniture was built in, and all of the storage was, so they simply didn't need the bureaux and wooden boxes and chests that had held cookware and towels and clothing in their other homes. The result was a clean, bare elegance that made Gaby feel empty-hearted.

The night after they moved Lily's furniture from the guest room into the living room, she'd lain in bed, excitedly thinking of how she might have it upholstered once the old woman had left, and remembering the profusion of dark objects and bric-à-brac in her family's house outside Paris, walking again in her mind through the maze of tables and chairs and screens and little desks at her grandmother's house in the country.

Now she was thinking of the other architects they knew, of their houses, uncluttered and serene for the most part. Messy lives, though. Gaby had always suspected that this was more true for architects than for other professional groups. It was their lack of schedule, she had often thought. Their working days were fluid, changeable, full of people and the whims of people. Full of women. Look at Alan: what would he do today? He had a house being built, so he'd probably drop over there and make sure it was going well, perhaps be in touch with the clients – the owners – if there were problems to work out. He was hoping for at least two other projects that Gaby knew about, a little church in Vermont (money was the question there), and a big elaborate addition onto one of the old houses in the village. So there would be time in the office, time on the telephone, maybe coffee or lunch or a drink with someone or other, charming them, amusing them, persuading them that this or that detail or surface or type of window was worth the extra cost in terms of what it would give back to them. Persuasion. Aesthetic conversions. Seduction, really. And it was more often the women than the men who cared, who had to be persuaded. Perhaps that was how architects got into trouble.

Gaby sighed. They'd had their share of trouble certainly. And made it through. Though Gaby, not Alan, had been the cause of the last crisis, with her affair. And this house, as she well knew, was a seduction too, meant to win her back. She was to have fallen in love with Alan again.

'*Don't*,' she had wanted to say. 'You don't need to.'

He had needed to though. And she supposed in a certain way it had worked. She did love the house, and he believed in that love. What he might not have believed was that she'd never stopped loving him, though this was true.

It wasn't Gaby's first affair. She'd had one much earlier in their marriage too, before the children were born. Alan had never known about that one. It had happened at a time of difficulty between them anyway, when Alan himself was having multiple lovers – though they carefully spoke of it then as an 'open marriage,' rather than infidelity.

No, Gaby's real lover, as she thought of him, had come along two years before the house. She hadn't told Alan about it until it was over. And then, foolishly, she had thought she could present it as a kind of fait accompli, a reason for having been withdrawn temporarily, and sad. One day, making dinner, she had simply announced it to Alan, that it had happened and now was done with.

He had been shocked, and then outraged. He had walked away from her, stood with his back to her at the window. Then, abruptly, he'd lifted his arm and the glass exploded.

There'd been blood everywhere. Gaby had grabbed a clean towel and wrapped it tightly around Alan's hand. She'd called to the boys, told them to finish fixing dinner, to clean up, that she didn't know when she and Alan would be back. She'd driven him to the clinic.

After that, there was the wait, not knowing whether Alan's hand would recover. There were Alan's questions too, which Gaby tried not to answer. She didn't want to talk about it, she told him. She didn't want to play twenty questions.

Alan did, of course. And slowly he found out most of what he wanted to know.

The man was much younger than Gaby, someone she'd met in the shop – he stopped in for morning coffee and a roll each day. She had thought they would sleep together perhaps once or twice. She'd supposed because he was younger, 'and quite attractive,' she told Alan, that all he was interested in her for was a quick affair.

She reminded Alan that he'd been away a good deal right then, that he'd had that project in Dallas.

Dallas. Dallas had been eight months earlier. 'So this, this affair, which has fairly recently ended, began eight months ago.'

Well, yes, she said. But it ended two months ago. And now, no more questions.

But Alan couldn't let go of it. *Six months!* For six months then, everything had been a lie. Every good moment between him and Gaby. All of it was going on while Gaby thought of someone else, wanted to be with someone else.

It wasn't like that, she said. Not at all.

Then what was it like, he wanted to know. What was it like when she made love with *her friend*? What was it like when she made love with Alan in that time?

And then all the other questions. Who was he? What did he do? Where did they go to be together? How often? Did he come to the shop anymore?

Gaby tried to put him off, but as he discovered, when he asked a question that called for a simple yes or no answer, she felt somehow honor-bound to respond. When he asked what they did together sexually, her lips tightened and she turned away from him, but there was a lot he could find out with another kind of question.

She caught his gaze on her often, appraising, trying to gauge her attractiveness to someone else, she supposed. Someone younger. She had grown a little heavier through the years, though

33

she wasn't plump or fat. She was solid, solid and wide. She had a short, strong body that looked better naked, actually, than it did clothed.

It was early spring when she'd told him about the affair. One day in late summer when it seemed his hand was going to be all right again, she'd come into the house they were living in then, the old, ramshackle house they'd bought in the village. She'd been watering the garden. She was wearing a bikini. She was barefoot, and her feet were wet and flecked with blades of grass. She'd browned everywhere, as she liked to do in summer, and her short, curling hair was damp at her forehead and her neck.

She had a story to tell Alan. A young couple had been walking past the house just now, teenagers. Their neighbor had mowed his field earlier in the day, and the sweet smell of the fresh grass was everywhere. 'Christ,' the girl had said to the boy, 'don't you just *hate* the smell of new-mown hay?'

Gaby was laughing as she repeated this, and Alan laughed too. Then he stopped and looked hard at her, at her body, at her legs and feet, and she knew what he was thinking of. After a long moment, he asked his last question. 'So, you're done with him. That's it.'

Gaby paused and then sighed. She had wanted to spare him this hurt, and herself the hurt of revealing it. But now she said wearily, 'My dear, I would say, on the contrary, that he was quite done with me. But that *is* it.'

She heard him inhale sharply, but he turned away before she could see his response. They never talked about the affair again. He had nothing more to ask.

JANE SMILEY

Moo

Jane Smiley is one of America's greatest contemporary writers, the winner of the Pulitzer Prize for her last novel, *A Thousand Acres*. In this, her eighth work of fiction, she has written a witty and delectable comedy of manners, set in Moo University, an agricultural college deep in the wheatfields of the American Midwest. Jane Smiley turns her wryly perceptive eye towards a community where men and women, the innocent and the cynical, thinkers and careerists, live and work together – in total disharmony . . .

'*Moo* slips down a treat, a long, refreshing read with a sweet aftertaste. A brilliantly funny read.'

AISLING FOSTER, Independent on Sunday

Jane Smiley is the author of eight works of fiction, including *Barn Blind*, *Ordinary Love*, and the highly acclaimed, best-selling *A Thousand Acres*.

MARCH   £6.99   PAPERBACK

Moo

HELEN LEVY GAVE a dinner party every weekend. She had big copper pots with silver lids hanging above the six-burner range, and large brightly colored bowls and stacks of big platters and two soup kettles, four-gallon and eight-gallon, and a table with three leaves that could seat up to twenty, and she had windows all along the length of the tiled kitchen counters that looked out upon her herb garden and her vegetable garden and her edible-flower garden. Instead of her former husband, who had cost her a lot of money, she had a man who helped in the garden who cost much less. She had a desk in the kitchen. She had cookbooks in French and Italian, including Vietnamese and Moroccan cookbooks in French and Ethiopian cookbooks in Italian. She had written one book in the old days, when one book was enough for a full professorship and since then she had confined herself to gustatorial research into recipes, kitchen techniques, and cooking equipment. She would never publish again, but most assuredly, given her root cellar, freezer, and food dryer, neither would she perish.

Guest lists came to her in dreams, and this week she had dreamed up seven possibilities – Cecelia Sanchez, who needed to be introduced around; Timothy Monahan, who seemingly did not need to be introduced to Cecelia; Ivar Harstad, whose relationship with Helen was as discreet as it was long-standing; Dean Jellinek, who lived next door and worked in Animal Science; his girlfriend, Joy, who was about five feet tall and as big around as a baseball bat (Equine Management); Margaret Bell, whom Helen was growing more and more fond of the longer they sat on that horrible tenure committee; and Dr. Bo Jones, whose relationship with Helen had ended fourteen years earlier, but who loved the bouillabaisse Helen was serving, and whose wife, Carla, Helen's good friend, was away visiting their daughter and her new baby. Only Dean and Joy formed an actual pair, so only they were having trouble getting along. One of Helen's principles was never to invite more than one couple for every six singles, ever since the birthday party she had given for her former husband where each of the four couples invited had squabbled on the road and turned back, leaving Helen and Howard to eat all of the osso buco and the chocolate fondue by themselves, an extended interaction that had led them into a fight, as well.

Helen didn't mind if a dinner party wasn't successful. There were so many of them, after all, and the food was always good, but this party had gone well, all the way through the frozen raspberry mousse and chocolate-dipped orange wafers she was now clearing from the table. Dr. Bo had been discoursing about hogs, which allowed the other guests to ruminate peacefully and think their own thoughts, when Margaret broke in suddenly and exclaimed, 'You know, this reminds me of something I hadn't thought of in years. Before I ever went to school, we used to go to my great-grandparents' place in the country, and it seems like everybody there lived in terror of the hogs. I remember there was a mule and also a horse, and if we rode them into the woods, we had to be careful to never fall off, because then the hogs would get us. It seems to me that we were told they would eat us. Are hogs carnivorous?'

Dr. Bo pressed himself back in his chair until it creaked, and said, 'Hungry hog'll eat almost anything. Used to be common practice to let 'em forage in the woods, and the veneer of civilization lies very lightly on the hog, very lightly indeed. You say to that hog, "Adapt," and that hog will adapt, whether to a life of ease or a life of brutish warfare. All over the world, hog and human take each other's measure. It is a delicate alliance, as your folks would have attested.'

Swept up in her newly discovered train of memory, Margaret said, 'And back home, we never had pork. My father couldn't stand pork!'

'Where are you from?' said Joy.

'I grew up in Kansas City, but all of my father's family lived in Arkansas. That's where those hogs were. I think I was only five the last time we visited there.'

Dean said, 'I'm surprised you remember it. My family moved when I was five, and I can go right to the house we lived in before and not recall a thing.'

Dr. Bo, not to be turned from his favorite subject, said, 'That hog, that southern hog, would have been lean and very fast. Rich in the hams, dark in the shoulder.'

Margaret said, 'My grandmother did bring the ham to the table as if – you know, she always said, "Jesus himself ate ham at the Last Supper," and my uncle always said, "Jews don't eat ham, Mama," and then my grandmother would look at him and say, "Well, how do you think they knew he was a Christian and not a Jew, then?"'

Everybody laughed.

Dr. Bo tried for one last fact. 'Spanish brought the hog, set 'em free all over the Caribbean so they could come back the next year to a ready food supply. Ecological disaster, of course.' Helen set a cup of coffee in front of him, and he drank deeply of it.

There was a long pause in the conversation, not unusual when Dr. Bo was a member of the party. Helen knew that most of the guests were trying to develop some interest in, and feeling for, the information they had just been given about hogs. She said, 'Shall we take our coffee into the living room?" Twenty minutes left, a half an hour at the most, even though it was only ten-thirty. This group was predominantly youthful, and that meant sobriety. She looked across at Ivar. In her first year at the university, they had met at a party given by a couple in the psychology department where the whiskey drinking, as at all parties then, started at six, dinner was brought to the table toward ten, and heads were

39

sometimes laid upon the table between courses. The last drop of brandy was licked from the rim of the last bottle long after midnight. At that particular party, in fact, the hostess's elderly mother, bourbon in hand, was discovered, along about nine, to have passed away in her chair. She was left to herself, just her legs covered with an afghan and the drink removed from her grasp, until the roast beef and coffee could sober everyone up. Helen had been impressed by the aplomb with which the hostess had gazed down at her mother, thoughtfully sipped her own drink, then returned to the kitchen and taken the rolls from the oven.

Timothy Monahan accepted brandy, turned the glass in his palm, and looked at Cecelia, who had seated herself beside Joy Pfisterer. The problem, he was tempted to think (but thinking this way was always a temptation), was that his fame didn't penetrate here, and so couldn't work in his favor, for example with Cecelia, the way it did out East. The stories in *Granta* and *The Paris Review*, the pieces in *7 Days*, even the reviews he'd done for *The Times* meant nothing here. They didn't speak nearly as much for him as the bad review he'd gotten (with picture) in *People* magazine spoke against him. After that appearance, eleven of his students had mentioned that their mothers had wondered if Timothy Monahan were him? With such a review, you were tempted to say no, the short answer, or to explain the difference in America between high culture and low culture, the long answer. At any rate, just to use the scientific method, this summer, his triumphal progress from writers' conference to writers' conference had proved sexual as well as professional, and there they knew his name beforehand and here he had to explain to every new acquaintance that he was in the English department and what he did there, often to be greeted by polite 'Hmms' as if even an explanation weren't enough to establish his identity. Apparently Cecelia had been so immersed in her courses and dissertation that her ignorance of his work was as total as anyone's. In this flirtation he was conducting, he had had to rely entirely on his personality, never a good idea.

Margaret sat down beside him and took a sip of his brandy. He said, 'Hey, kiddo.'

She said, 'I haven't had much of a chance to talk to you tonight. Did you put together your review materials?'

'I turned them in Thursday. But you aren't going to see them for months, right?'

'I'm not going to see them. As a member of your department, I have no input at all.'

'Well, that's probably for the best, eh, Dr. Bell?'

'Oh, I don't know.' She smiled, possibly with some affection – Tim couldn't tell. His affair with Margaret, three years in the past now, had been firmly grounded in his understanding that she had never read any of his work. Then, one Sunday over breakfast and *The Times*, she had made a little noise, one little noise, at a review of the third novel by a writer he knew and detested, a total fraud whose whole approach to the novel was unserious in the extreme, whose style was second-rate and had been since Tim had known him at Columbia. It was an appreciative noise, so Tim had looked up, said, 'What?' and Margaret had pointed out the review, and Tim had snorted, and then Margaret had said she was including a paper about this joker in her book, and Tim had said, 'Well, in that case, you really OUGHT to read my work,' and she had said, 'I have, you know that,' and they had looked at one another and he had never felt an iota of desire for her afterward; try as he might, all the unspoken opinions that had changed hands in those few minutes still shrivelled him right up, it wasn't even vengeful. He smiled and said, 'Well, there is a conflict of interest.'

She nodded, and said, 'Did you sell your new book yet?'

'It's at Little, Brown, now.'

'A sale would make a big difference. With three, you'd be in there absolutely. No amount of ignorance or perplexity on their part would matter at all.'

Tim shrugged. 'A sale would make a big difference' was his life's watchword right now.

'I'll be back.' Margaret stood up and headed toward the bathroom.

Cecelia stretched and yawned, touched her hair to see if the pins were falling out. The gesture lifted her breasts, which were large, and marvelously concentrated his attention on the loose white cotton of her blouse. He heard her say, 'Actually, I walked. My duplex is only a few blocks.'

Before Joy could say a word, he was in there. 'Say, I walked, too, I'd be glad to walk you home.' Fleeting amusement crossed her features, but she said, 'All right, Tim.'

He said to Joy, 'We teach in adjacent rooms.'

Cecelia said, 'Yes, and his class is always laughing and my class is always droning.'

'Well, they read their work aloud to each other, and they find themselves very funny.'

Joy looked at him in a serious way. He said to her, 'What do you do?'

'Right now, we're on parasites. Next week, inoculations.'

'Of what?'

'Oh. Of horses. And I manage the university's horse herd and run the riding club.' She fell silent, still looking at him. Clearly she was a person for whom conversation was not an end in itself. He returned her gaze for a while, then said, 'Well, Cecelia, let me know when you're ready to go.'

He picked up his coffee cup and looked into it, then drank a sip. The party was winding down, and there wasn't much left to do. He had schmoozed with the provost twice already, complimented Helen on the food, listened to the Jellinek guy go on and on about bovine cloning and the vet guy do hogs. He had contemplated how he might fit Margaret's early childhood recollections, which were certainly picturesque, into something he might write, and he had noted, on his visit to the bathroom, which was upstairs, the drugs Helen was taking or had taken, the names of the cosmetics she bought in France, the price of a new sweater she'd left lying on her bed. He had opened her bathroom closet

42

and noted boxes of tampons, which meant she hadn't gone through menopause yet, and a couple of diaphragm cases, ditto, with the additional implication that she was still sexually active. The rumors were that her sexual activity had once been various and unstinting. Tim was glad to see that cooking hadn't replaced that. Tim was glad, in fact, to see any evidence of sexual activity at all around the university. Every so often he wondered, with a touch of self-consciousness, if he were not a solitary toiler in that particular cabbage patch. There were other, much more interesting rumors about Helen, too, ones that gave you to contemplate age-old philosophical questions. Tim sat, staring at his brandy, contemplating these questions, until he had finished it.

After that, he smiled at the provost, who smiled back in that knowing but secretive way of his, and then Cecelia said, for him to hear, 'Well, I guess –' and Helen said, 'Must you –' and that was that.

Dr. Dean Jellinek, Animal Science, and his great and good friend, Joy Pfisterer, walked silently to his house next door, as befitted a couple who had been arguing for three days, and had only set aside their differences for the evening in the interests of appearance. He let them in and turned off the porch light, glancing toward the upstairs, which was dark. Joy said, 'Chris must have gone to bed after all. I don't hear the TV.' They stood in silence, listening.

'I'll check the computer room in a minute. Are you going home or staying?'

'I have to get up at five.'

'People get up at five around here. Other people sleep right through it.'

'It's easier –'

'Fine, call me as soon as you get in the house.'

'Dean –'

'Joy. Stoshie isn't around anymore. I don't like you going into an empty apartment.' The apartment wasn't yet empty, Joy thought. There were still almost two weeks before she would be moving into Dean's large and pleasant house.

'There's so much to do before the new renters move in over there, I just –'

None of these topics were the source of their disagreement, but clearly, thought Joy, anything could be sucked right in, even Stoshie, her elderly Dalmatian, whom she had put to sleep a month before (kidney failure). Joy put her hand on the doorknob. 'Give Chris a good-night kiss for me.'

'The provost thinks funding is likely. A lot of funding. A couple million for exploratory research.'

'Great.' Now they were right in it.

'He named four or five sources right off, a couple that I hadn't thought of. There could be real speed.'

'Good. Speed is good.'

'Joy –'

'What?'

'I need your support on this. This is going to make up for the other.'

'You've got to get over the other anyway, without anything making up for it.'

'I can't. You know perfectly well that now, forever, they'll call it the Dichter Technique. It could have been called the Jellinek Technique.'

'But he doesn't own that technique! You don't have to pay him to use it –'

'People who have put their lifeblood into developing something just work their lives away in obscurity while someone else rises to the top.'

Cloning. Cloning. Dean was obsessed with cloning, and wore his obsession for all to see. It was true that he had put his life's blood, or, at least, ten years of work and money from lots of grants, into working out a technique for the transfer of nuclear material from one calf embryo to another by placing the two eight-cell calf embryos between two electrodes, turning on the

44

juice, and thereby causing the embryos to become one, though Joy was not quite clear on exactly how this happened. And it was also true that Dean had been writing up his article on these successful nuclear transfers, fussing a bit over his style, thinking he had an edge, some publication leeway, when, lo and behold, Dichter et al. from UC Davis had blindsided him with an article in *Nature*. That was in the spring. Since then, Dean had sat around the house, bemoaning all the conferences he hadn't managed to attend, all the minute ways in which it must be that he wasn't quite in the loop – he hadn't heard a word, no one had told him a thing – though he was sure everyone knew, his grad students, his colleagues, his connections at the FDA, the editors at all the journals he published in. But now he had come up with a new idea and Joy had made the mistake of showing skepticism and he had been mad at her for three days.

It was a great idea, simple in the way of all great ideas, as cloning was a simple idea. Cloning, Dean had often told her, came to everyone slightly differently. It had come to him years before, the story went, when Chris was just a baby watching Saturday morning cartoons. They'd been sitting together on the couch, eating father-son bowls of Rice Krispies, and it had come on TV, one image of a puppy that suddenly reproduced itself into a drill team. They barked, they wagged their tails, they turned their heads, all together, and just then he, Dean Jellinek, had seen cows, beautiful black and white Holsteins in a green pasture, all marked the same, all turning their heads, all mooing, all switching their tails, all in unison, a clone herd, the perfect herd of perfect cows. Why would you do it, he thought just then, and the answer was simple, too, always the sign of a good answer: you would do it because it was beautiful and because you COULD do it.

He had staggered to his feet with the beauty and simplicity of it, and set down his cereal bowl on the couch, where Elaine's elderly schnauzer had taken care of the cleanup. He had staggered out of the house and gotten into his car to go to the lab, leaving Chris by himself without even realizing it. Elaine had returned from the supermarket to find the two-year-old hard at work adjusting the reception dials on the TV so that every channel received only static.

But the picture in his mind! Green meadow, blue sky, identical black and white cows all turning their heads toward him at the same time with the same gesture! Divorce, custody, solitude, new love, all had intervened between that time and this, but desire propelled him insistently, relentlessly, toward this picture. Then Dichter et al. came along, and it was very much like watching the only woman you ever loved marry another man and take his name, except that, in Dean's personal opinion, there were many potential wives, but only one or two simple great ideas.

Joy reached up and pulled his head down for a good-night kiss. He was stiff, and wouldn't bend. She smiled in a teasing way, and said, 'Come on. We'll see. Don't be mad anymore. I hate not getting along. Anyway, it's not me you have to convince, it's the people with the money. You're a great grant proposal writer.'

'Am I?' He knew she would say yes.

'You are. I have faith in YOU. It's just an unusual idea to me. I'll get used to it.'

He was mollified. He bent down and gave her a long, warm kiss. He whispered, 'It could work.'

Meanwhile, Tim's flirtation with Cecelia was progressing better than he suspected, and better than Cecelia considered wise. The fact was that he was very good-looking in THAT WAY (as Cecelia described it to herself), and when she got up on the mornings of their adjacent class meetings, she dressed more carefully and with more pleasure, she felt less of the tedium of routine, and the day before her seemed shorter in prospect. Her sense of the quiet around her had not diminished, had induced in her an answering sleepiness. When she mentioned this to her father on the phone, he had reminded her of her first day in first grade – the room had been so quiet in contrast to kindergarten that she had fallen asleep at her desk and then fallen out of her chair and been sent home.

After that, her academic career had more or less prospered, until now. The students drilled industriously, but in a kind of murmur. One time she had instructed them to shout their answers, but after three or four they had subsided, embarrassed, into the drone they were comfortable with. Other days, she made them walk around and address one another conversationally; she made them pretend to argue or to haggle; she saw at once that they would back down in any conflict, be suckered in any market transaction, and that they considered their reticence a form of becoming modesty. Little did they know that they were putting her to sleep, that she could not remember any of their names, that she had less interest in them than in any group she had ever taught.

Nor were her colleagues much better. They invited her for dinner or lunch, but there seemed to be a general taboo against introducing any remotely unpleasant subject in the presence of food. And everything at all real was deemed unpleasant: the fact that her father, a doctor in Mexico, was a gardener in Los Angeles, and her mother, an accountant in Mexico, was a bookkeeper; interethnic conflict in L.A. in general; her divorce; the association of one of her cousins with an L.A. street gang – the kind response of any intercolutor when she stumbled upon one of these subjects was to assume that she must be ashamed to talk about such things and to relieve her of the necessity. Departmental conflicts, which were many, it turned out, were spoken of only by allusion and only in low voices. Whenever Cecelia felt she was showing a flattering interest in the personal lives of her new acquaintances, they said, 'Oh, you can't want to hear about that, it's so ordinary.' When, in the departmental office, she happened to eavesdrop upon others' conversations, they were invariably talking about gardening, remodelling, or problems in the schools, three subjects she could not have been less curious about. One signal conversation, which she had lingered near for ten minutes, between two woman German professors, had concerned a support group they both belonged to for people with an overwhelming compulsion to tear up their clothes and braid them into rag rugs.

In this dreamy sea of quietude, Timothy Monahan stood out, would have stood out even if he had not looked THAT WAY (black hair, blue eyes, thin face, large hands). He was not direct and volatile like the men she had grown up with, but everything he said, and he said a lot, was inviting. It invited laughter or disagreement or outrage, even, or sex, or thought, but it always invited some response, and promised that all responses were interesting, worth his attention. Cecelia knew (thus her caution) that this habit of his was not any more a moral virtue than the face was, or the natural physical grace. She had mistaken qualities of style for elements of character before, and clearly she was disoriented and vulnerable, and he sensed that and that was another reason to be cautious. Look at him. Right now, walking down the street, he was inviting disbelief. 'You know,' he said, 'she has two vaginas.'

'You can't know that.'

'I swear.'

'She's told you that?'

'Two complete sets of female reproductive organs.'

'I'm offended that you should tell me this.'

'Don't you think it's enhancing? I do.' He smiled wickedly at her.

'I think it's her business, not mine or yours.'

'It's interesting.'

'I'm going to put this out of my mind as soon as we stop talking about it.'

'Why? It's just an anatomical fact.'

'How naive of you to say so.'

'You were in her kitchen. You saw all those giant bowls and pots and pasta servers and flower planters and colanders and orchids and that big red amaryllis and the Georgia O'Keeffe reproduction on the wall. It's the theme of her life, but it's still just an anatomical fact. I think of it as a kind of test. I'm sure some people are quite uncomfortable at her parties. I happen to be extraordinarily comfortable. It just depends on how you feel about women. But everybody knows.'

'Everybody *believes*. Belief is never knowledge, no matter how strongly held.'

'Some know, then. And some of them have told.'

'I don't know.' Cecelia knew she sounded snappish. She glanced at Tim. He couldn't suppress a smile. 'You're teasing me!'

He shrugged. 'Interesting idea, though, isn't it?'

'You'll say anything.'

'Maybe.'

Her porch loomed. She stopped in the street. 'Thank you for walking me home.'

'Hey.' He grasped her wrist and drew her toward him.

She removed his hand. 'I don't like being teased.'

'It's true, then.'

'Then I don't like that sort of gossip.'

'It's a game, then. Like writing a novel. A game of meditating over objects of the imagination.'

'You can't come onto my porch, and don't try to kiss me. I'm annoyed with you, and I hate it if men find that arousing.'

'Okay. But I will watch you in the door.'

'Okay.'

'Then I'll walk back to Helen's and get my car.' As always, he spoke with playful equanimity. She turned on her heel, mounted the porch steps with dignity, and jammed her key into the lock. He shouted, 'Night, Cecelia. I'll call you tomorrow!' as if he didn't care whether he woke up the whole neighborhood. Cecelia winced at the noise bursting in the silence, maybe for the first time ever.

DORIS LESSING

Love, Again

Julie Vairon was a lovely and wayward French girl from Martinique, living in Provence at the end of the nineteenth century. She was a musician, a diarist, an artist, a 'free woman' ahead of her time. Nearly eighty years after her death in 1912, her music and her art illuminate the lives of the characters of *Love, Again*, when Sarah Durham, a theatrical producer, commissions a play based on Julie's life. The play captivates all who come into contact with it, and dramatically changes the lives of everyone involved. For Sarah – an old woman – the change is profound; she falls in love with two younger men, one after the other.

Doris Lessing's first novel since 1988, *Love, Again* is one of the most compelling and memorable she has ever written.

Doris Lessing has won many literary prizes, among them the Prix Medici, the Austrian State Prize for European Literature, the German Federal Republic Shakespeare Prize, the W.H. Smith Literary Award and the James Tait Black Memorial Prize.

APRIL   £15.99   HARDBACK

Love, Again

SHE WOKE, PROBABLY because the music had at last been switched off. Silence. Not quite; the cicadas still made their noise . . . no, it was not cicadas. The spray had been left to circle its rays of water all night on the dusty grass under the pine tree, and its click, click, clicking sounded like a cicada. The moon was a small yellow slice low over the town roofs. Dusty stars, the smell of watered dust. Down on the pavement outside the now closed café, two figures stretched out side by side in chairs brought close together. Low voices, then Bill's loud young laugh. From that laugh she knew it was not a girl with him: he would not laugh like that with Molly, with Mary – with any woman.

Sarah went back to her bed and lay awake, tormented, on the top of the sheet. The breath of the night was hot, for the water being flung about down there was not doing much to cool things off. It occurred to her she was feeling more than desire: she could easily weep. What for?

Sarah dreamed. Love is hot and wet, but it does not scald and sting. She woke as a phantom body – a body occupying the same space as hers – slid away and separated, becoming small. This baby body had been soaked in a stinging hot wetness and was filled with a longing so violent the pain of it fed back into her own body. She turned and bit the pillow. The taste of dry cotton embittered her tongue.

She lay flat on her back and saw that a street light made patterns on her ceiling. A late car's headlights plunged the ceiling into day and left it modelled with shadow. There were voices outside in the corridor. One was Stephen's, the other a girl's, very low. If

53

that was Molly, well then, good luck to them both: this blessing, she knew, was well over the top.

Her eyes were not, it seemed, entirely bound by this room but were still attending to the dream, or to another, for a world of dreams lay around her and she was immersed in them, and yet could observe her immersion. Very close was that region where the baby in her lived. She could feel its desperation. She could feel the presence of other entities. She saw a head, young, beautiful, Bill's (or Paul's), smiling in self-love, gazing into a mirror, but it turned with a proud and seductive slowness, and the head was not a man's but a girl's, a fresh good-looking girl whose immediately striking quality was animal vitality. This girl turned away her confident smile, and she dissolved back into a young man. Sarah put her hands up to her own face, but what her fingers lingered over was her face now. Beneath that (so temporary) mask were the faces she had had as a young woman, as a girl, and as a baby. She wanted to get up and go to the glass to make certain of what was there, but felt held to the bed by a weight of phantom bodies that did not want to be flushed out and exposed. At last she did get herself out of bed and to the window. The chairs on the pavement were empty. The square was empty. The hard little moon had gone behind black roofs. The forgotten water spray swung around, click, click, click.

There were words on her tongue. She was saying, '. . . passing the stages of her age and youth, entering the whirlpool . . . yes, that's it, the whirlpool,' said Sarah, not sure whether she was awake or asleep. Was she really sitting by the window? Yes, she was fully awake, but her tongue kept offering her, '. . . stages of my age and youth, entering the whirlpool.'

She was dissolved in longing. She could not remember ever feeling the rage of want that possessed her now. Surely never in her times of being in love had she felt this absolute, this peremptory need, an emptiness that hollowed out her body, as if life itself was being withheld from her.

Who is it that feels this degree of need, of dependence, and who has to lie helpless waiting for the warm arms and the moment of being lifted up into love?

It was four o'clock. The light would come into the square in an hour or so. She showered. She dressed, taking her time, and, ready for her day, went back to the window. The tops of the trees went pink, and light poured over the still unpeopled town. An old woman came down rue Julie Vairon and into the square. She wore a long-sleeved cotton dress, white, with a pattern of small mauve bouquets, and black collar and cuffs. Her white hair was in a bun. She walked slowly, careful where she put her feet. She sat herself on the bench underneath the plane tree, first brushing the dust off carefully with a large white handkerchief. She sat listening to the sound of the sprayer, and to the cicadas when they started. When the birds began, she smiled. She liked being alone in the square. She did not know Sarah watched her from her window. Her mother had probably sat there on that bench, alone in the early morning. Her grandmother too, thinking cruel thoughts about Julie.

Sarah let herself out of her room, went down the stairs. No one yet at reception. She slid back the bolt on the hotel's main door and was on the pavement. As she went past, she sent a smile to the old woman, who nodded and smiled at her. 'Bonjour, Madame.' 'Bonjour, Madame.'

Julie's house in the hills was about three miles away. Sarah took her time, because it was already hot. Pink dust lay along the edges of the tarmac, reddened the tree trunks and the foliage. Leaves drooped, made soft by a long absence of rain. The sun stood up over the hills and filled the rough pine trunks with red light and laid shadow under the bushes. Julie's landscape was an ungiving one, dry and austere, nothing like the forests of her Martinique where the flowers' perfumes were heavy, narcotic. Here there were the brisk scents of thyme and oregano and pine. The tarmac had ended. Sarah walked where Julie had, thinking of all that separated her from the woman who had died over eighty years before. By the time she reached the house, hot air was dragging at her skin.

Already two young men were at work setting chairs to rights and picking up the detritus of last night's concert. This empty place, surrounded by old trees, seemed the proper stage for ancient and inexorable dramas, as if onto it would walk a masked player to announce the commencement of a tale where the Fates pursued their victims, and where gods bargained with each other over favours for their protégés. Interesting to imagine Julie's little tale being discussed by Aphrodite and Athene. Sarah walked past Julie's house, now burdened with cables and loudspeakers, thinking about why one could only imagine these two goddesses like bossy headmistresses discussing a girl with a propensity for disorder. ('She could do much better if she tried.') Yet if Julie was not a 'love woman', then what was she? She had embodied that quality, recognizable by every woman at first glance, and at once felt by men, of the seductive and ruthless femininity that at once makes arguments about morality irrelevant – surely that should be Aphrodite's argument? But the woman who had written the journals, whose daughter was she?

I tell you, Julie, had said Julie to herself, something like ninety years before Sarah walked slowly in the hot morning away from her house towards the river, *if you let yourself love this man then it will be worse for you than it was with Paul. For this one is not a handsome boy who could only see himself when he was reflected in your eyes. Rémy is a man, even if he is younger than I am. With him it will be all my possibilities as a woman, for a woman's life, brought to life. And then, Julie? A broken heart is one thing, and you have lived through that. But a broken life is another, and you can choose to say no.* She did not say no. And who was it, which Julie, who said to the other, *Well, my dear, you must not imagine if you choose love you won't have to pay for it*? But it was not Athene's daughter who said, *Write your music. Paint your pictures. But if that is what you choose, you will not be living as women live. I can't endure this non-life. I can't endure this desert.*

Now just ahead was the river, with its pools and its shallow falls, and the bench the town authorities had thoughtfully provided for people who wanted to contemplate Julie's sad end. Someone was already on the bench. It was Henry. The curve of his body suggested discouragement. He stared ahead of him, and it was not because he was deaf that he did not hear her approach. His ears were plugged with sound. He had a Walkman in his pocket. The music he was listening to was sure to be as far as it could be from Julie's. Sarah could hear a frantic tiny niggling, then a small savage howling, as she sat down and smiled at him. He tore off the headphones, and as the music, no longer directed into his brain, swirled about them, he switched the machine off, looking embarrassed. He sang at her, '*Tell me what love means to you before you ask me to love you*' – Julie's words, but it was a tune she did not know, since she was not an inhabitant of the world he entered when he clamped his headphones on.

Then he put back his head and howled like a wolf.

She suggested, 'I am baying at the moon, for 'tis a night in June, and I'm thinking of you . . . of who? Of you-hoo.'

'Not bad. Not far off.'

'Have you been here all night?'

'Just about.'

'But you know it's going to be all right.'

He sang, 'Have you been here all night, but you know it's going to be all right.' He said, 'Yes, I know, but do I believe it?' He abruptly flung his legs apart, and his arms, then, finding this position intolerable, he threw the left leg over the right, then the right over the left, and folded his arms tight. A bright blowing spray set a bloom of cool damp on their faces. The river ran fast through the forest trees, past reddish and orange rocks, making baby whirlpools and eddies, leaving stains of pinkish foam on the weeds that oscillated at the river's edge. Above the fall was a wide pool where the water was dark and still, except where the main stream ran through it, betraying itself in a swift turbulence that gathered the whole body of water into itself at the rocky edge, flinging up spray as it fell into another pool, where it seethed like boiling sugar syrup among black rocks. This was not a deep pool, though it was the famous whirlpool that had drowned Julie and – so some of the townspeople said – had drowned Julie's child. (How could they have said it? Had there not been a doctor and the doctor's certificate? But if people want to believe something, they will.) Below this treacherous pool, past a mild descent among rocks, was another, large, dark, and quiet except where the water poured deeply into it. It was this pool where Julie came to swim, but only at night, when, she said, she could cheat the Peeping Toms.

'To drown herself there must have needed a real strength of mind,' said Sarah.

'She was probably stoned.'

'She never mentioned drinking or drugs in her journals.'

'Did she say everything in her journals?'

'I think so.'

'Then I'll go back to my first interpretation. When I read the script I didn't believe in the suicide.'

'You mean, you agree with the townspeople? They thought she was murdered.'

'Perhaps they murdered her.'

'But she was just about to become a respectable woman.'

'That's just the point. Suppose they didn't like the idea of this witch becoming Madame Master Printer.'

'A witch, you keep saying.'

'Do you know what, Sarah? I dream about her. If I dreamed of some sugarplum all tits and bum, then that would be something, but I don't. I dream of her when she's – well, getting over the hill. Well over.'

She turned her head to see his smile, sour, a bit angry, and close to her face.

'Sex appeal isn't all bum and tits,' said she, returning his vulgarity to him.

He sat back, gave her an appreciative but still angry smile, and said, 'Well, yes, I'd say there was some truth in that. Of course, as a good American boy, I should only be admitting to nymphets, but yes, you're right.' He sprang to his feet, grabbed up her hand, kissed it. Her hand was wet with spray. 'Sarah . . . what can I say? I'm off to get some sleep. If I can. I've got a technical rehearsal at eleven. Roy is rehearsing the townspeople. And I've got the singers this afternoon. Will you be there? But why should you be?'

'If you want me to be.'

'Lazing on a sunny afternoon,' he sang to her. Then he pushed the plugs back into his ears and walked or, rather, ran off back towards Julie's house.

She went to the edge of the pool below the falls. The whirlpool, in fact. Here Julie must have stood, looking down at the dangerous waters, and then she jumped. Not much of a jump, perhaps six feet. The stony bottom of the pool could be glimpsed through eddies. She could easily have landed on her feet, then fallen forward, perhaps onto that rock, a smooth round one, and allowed herself to be sucked past the rock to the deeper pool. Allowed herself? She could swim, she said, like an otter.

Sarah felt she should turn her head, and did so. There was Stephen, staring at her from where he stood by the bench a few feet away. She went to the bench and sat down. He sat beside her.

'We are all up early,' she remarked.

'I haven't been to bed. I suppose I look it.' His clothes were crumpled, he smelled stale, and he wore his tragic mask. Again Sarah thought, I've never, never in my life felt anything like this – this is the grief you see on the faces of survivors of catastrophes, staring back at you from the television screens. 'I went walking with Molly last night,' he said. 'She very kindly agreed to come walking with me. We walked along some road or other. It was pretty dark under the trees.'

She could imagine it. A dark road. He could hardly see the girl who walked beside him under the trees. There had been that niggardly little moon. They had walked from one patch of dim light to another. Molly had been wearing a white cotton skirt and a tight white T-shirt. Patterns in black and white.

Sarah watched the racing water, for she could not bear to look at his face.

'Extraordinary, isn't it? I mean, what happens to one's pride. She kissed me. Well, I kissed her.' He waited. Then, 'Thanks for not saying it, Sarah.' Now she did cautiously turn her head. Tears ran down cheeks dragging with grief. 'I don't understand any of it. What can you say about a man of fifty who knows that nothing more magical ever happened to him than a kiss in the dark with . . . ?'

Sarah suppressed, At least you had a kiss. At that moment anything she felt seemed a selfish impertinence.

'I've missed out on all that,' she heard, but faintly. A breeze off the water was blowing his words away. 'I've had a dry life. I didn't know it until . . . Of course I've been in love. I don't mean that.' The wind, changing again, flung his words at her: 'What does it mean, saying that to hold one girl in your arms makes everything that ever happened to you dust and ashes?'

'Julie said something of the sort. About Rémy.' A silence, filled with the sound of water. For the second time that morning, she said, 'To drown herself must have taken some strength of mind.'

'Yes. If I'd been there . . .'

'You, or Rémy?'

'You don't understand. I am Rémy. I understand everything about him.'

'Were you a younger brother? I mean you, Stephen.'

'I have two older brothers. Not four, like Rémy. I don't know how important that is. What's important is . . . well, what could I have said to her to stop her killing herself?'

'Will you marry me?' suggested Sarah.

'Ah, you *don't* understand. That is the impossibility. He couldn't marry her. Not with all that pressure. Don't forget, he was French. It is a thousand times worse for the French than for us. The French have this family thing. We have it, but nothing like as bad. We can marry chorus girls and models – and a jolly good thing too. Good for the gene pool. But have you ever seen an aristocratic French family close ranks? And it was a hundred years ago. No, it was all inevitable. It was impossible for Rémy not to fall in love with her. And until death. Because he would have loved her all his life.'

'Yes,' she shouted, since the wind had changed again.

'But impossible to marry her.'

'Funny how we don't mention the glamorous lieutenant,' said Sarah, thinking of Bill and of how ashamed she was.

'But that was just . . . falling in love,' he shouted. A silence. He said, 'But with Rémy, it was life and death.'

He sat with his eyes shut. Tears seeped out under his lids. Depressed. But the word means a hundred different shades of sadness. There are different qualities of 'depression', as there are of love. A really depressed person, she knew, having seen the condition in a friend, was nothing like Stephen now. The depressed one could sit in the same position in a chair, or on the floor in a corner of a room, curled like a foetus for hours at a time. Depression was not tears. It was deadness, immobility. A black hole. At least, so it seemed to an onlooker. But Stephen was alive and suffering. He was grief-stricken. She cautiously examined him, now that she could, because he had his eyes shut, and thought suddenly that she ought to be afraid for herself. She, Sarah, had most unexpectedly stopped a bolt from the blue, an arrow from an invisible world: she had fallen in love when she thought she never could again. And so what was to stop her from being afflicted, as Stephen was – from coming to grief?

She took his hand, that sensible, useful, practical hand, and felt it tighten around hers. 'Bless you, Sarah. I don't know why you put up with me. I know I must seem . . .' He got up, and so did she. 'I think I ought to get some sleep.'

They walked to the edge of the dangerous pool and stood looking down. The water that spattered Sarah's cheek was partly tears blown off Stephen's.

'She must have taken a pretty strong dose of something.'

'That's what Henry said.'

'Did he? A good chap, Henry. Perhaps he's in love with her too. The way I feel now, I can't imagine why the whole world isn't. That's a sign of insanity in itself.'

The sun was burning down, though it was still early. Hot, quiet, and still. No wind. Sarah's dress, so recently put on, needed changing, for it was soaked with spray and clung to her thighs. She shut her eyes as she was absorbed into a memory of a small hot damp body filled with craving.

'Just as well we don't remember our childhoods,' she said.

RHIDIAN BROOK

The Testimony of Taliesin Jones

To eleven-year-old Taliesin Jones, God is as real as the fields of his father's farm, as palpable as the apple he buys daily on his way to school. In Cwmglum where he lives in rural West Wales, God is all around, even at school where Hoop The Mental hits him on the nose and earthy Julie Dyer both taunts and tempts him. Though it sets him apart, Taliesin's faith is his strength when his mother leaves home with her hairdresser, and when his father slips into a distracted gloom and his older brother turns from ally to surly adolescent. But it is with elderly Billy Evans, piano teacher and amateur healer, that Taliesin finds a source of miracles, miracles which transform his life . . .

Rhidian Brook originally comes from Tenby, South Wales. He now works part-time as a copywriter and lives with his wife in Chiswick. *The Testimony of Taliesin Jones* is his first novel.

APRIL   £9.99   HARDBACK

The Testimony of Taliesin Jones

TIME PASSES SLOWLY when you're waiting for the amazing to happen. It is two days now since Taliesin took his warts to Billy. Two wart-watching tenterhooking days spent waiting for a miracle, thinking about the as yet unanswered prayer. Billy told him to be patient, to wait on God – who is good to those who wait on Him. He said that God was a mover of warts and mountains alike, that there was no detail too small for Him to fix. God could have them disappear in a trice if He wanted to, or He might decide to bide His time. There was no telling. God worked to His own timing, not to the prearranged ticktocking of clocks and calendars or even the unseen changing of a Skin Clock. God was in the past, present and future all at the same time according to His will, he said.

In two days Taliesin's doubt has spread like pins and needles through his body, numbing his belief that something is going to happen. Last night, as he read and finished his book his eyes kept moving to his hands, hoping to find clean skin. The Eleven looked back at him, rude with health, challenging his belief. The largest and first wart at the end of his index finger transfigured to spokeswart and voiced the doubts. 'God's got more important things to do: the universe to sustain, the earth's turning to maintain, wars to sort out, the weather to organize, more serious illness to heal. What makes you think He's got time for us? You'll just have to let nature take its course. And anyway, it'll hardly count as a miracle. It's hardly water into wine is it? Miracles have to be instant don't they? If we go now it will be a perfectly natural thing. It'll be because of the vinegar you applied, not the prayer. God

65

had His chance to remove us in one supernatural go but He's avoided His opportunity. He hasn't answered you, has He?'

But Taliesin prays again and gives God a second chance to redeem himself. The miracle could still happen but for him to be sure God would have to make it clear, no half healing. Not one or two warts. All of them. Categorically, irrefutably, instantly.

Taliesin lies in bed and does deals with God. 'I won't keep it a secret if you heal them. No way. I'll tell the world about it. I'll tell them at school. I'll tell Hoop The Mental. I'll make sure my parents know. I'll try and heal people myself. I'll form a gang of healers – we'll lay hands on people. If you could just heal them tonight, please! Come on God, I know you're there, do it now!'

It is a Saturday morning. Still gloved, Taliesin is absently reading the back of a packet of oats. It says how food is our medicine, and that foods can cure a variety of ailments. Especially the oat. He helps himself to an extra bowlful. Jonathan is making himself scrambled eggs, singing a song that he likes. Now that he has a girlfriend he has started gelling his hair back in an attempt to look older.

'How much longer are you going to wear those gloves?' he asks, beating the eggs with one hand and swigging orange juice with the other.

'Until my warts have gone.'

'They won't help,' he says.

'I don't want them to spread, do I,' Taliesin says.

'I don't know how you can eat with them on. Why don't you go and see a doctor, get some pills or something.'

There are times when Taliesin wonders if Jonathan really can be his brother. He never reads, he's six feet tall, good at sport, a help to his father around the farm, vaguely handsome, he gells his hair, shaves, he's kissed a girl, and doesn't believe in God anymore. It is like sharing a house with his opposite; someone whose characteristics completely subtend his own. Their conversations are always a contrary, vice versa of wills and outlooks: Jonathan determined to gain the upper hand and abash his younger brother, Taliesin refusing to be put down. It is getting harder to find common ground. As they get older there are fewer things to talk about, the gap is widening, the games are changing, the field of mutual interest narrowing. These last two years Taliesin has understood this and strived to overcome it. He doesn't want to give up on his brother.

As he spoons his cereal he remembers the photograph of the Welsh rugby player on Billy Evans's piano.

'Mr Evans has got a photo of Spud Williamson on his piano. It's signed.'

Jonathan tries not to stop doing what he's doing but this is interesting.

'You can buy autographed pictures of players in the sports shop these days, they're not the real signatures,' he says, giving no ground.

'Spud's visited Mr Evans a few times to get his shoulder fixed.'

Jonathan puts the egg on some bread and half turns and listens as Taliesin continues to describe the photograph. 'He's wearing his Wales shirt and a funny hat with tassels.'

'You mean a cap. It's what you get for playing for your country.' Jonathan can't quite bring himself to ask why Mr Evans has a signed photograph of the player. 'I thought he taught piano.'

'He's a healer mainly. He spends most of his time doing that.'

Jonathan can't grasp this, and if he does, he doesn't want to show it. He shakes his head and forks in his egg. Taliesin makes some tea and pours his brother a mug even stirring in the sugar for him.

'Thanks.' To get a thank you out of Jonathan is a sweet thing and a sign of give. After a minute's silence he looks at his younger brother.

'So does he know Spud, then?'

'Yeah.'

Jonathan is impressed. 'Do you want to kick a ball around? We haven't had a game for ages. You can be Wales.' Jonathan becomes more animated now that sport is on the agenda. This offer is his way of continuing the conversation in a language he can use. He can submerge his dialogue in a game.

The garden is an oblong patch fenced in by a hedge. This is where small family dramas have been played out. It has been a battlefield, a tennis court, a temporary home for molly lambs, a space for drinking tea, sunbathing, hanging washing, a space where his mother once threw a full cup of coffee at his father (he never found out why), a space where Jonathan squashed ants, destroying hundreds with his finger, and a space where Taliesin lay down and read a book in one go.

The space has also staged a number of one-a-side rugby internationals (always Wales versus England). The hedge makes an even touchline and the leaves provide a densely packed crowd that roars when the wind is up. Not that they need the wind. When it comes to sport, real or simulacrum, Jonathan's imagination blossoms. He not only plays, he provides capacity-crowd sound effects, commentary and slow motion replays from three different angles. On the field of play his brother is quite a poet, purple in his commentary, prepared to imagine, happy to suspend disbelief, prepared to use a flashy simile and big metaphor, using words he'd never use in everyday conversation.

'The teams walk out into the crisp November air. The conditions are ideal for a running game and there is a little wind so kicking might prove problematic. After weeks of anticipation the two teams have finally come together in what many people believe will be one of the closest confrontations for years. Playing for Wales today is young Taliesin Jones, fresh from college and at eleven the youngest ever player to appear for the national team.'

It's Taliesin's turn to be Wales, which should mean a victory. Their matches are always superlative, close, and won in the last minute by a breathtaking, length-of-the-field move, involving the entire Welsh team. Being Wales means starting slowly while the English swagger into an early lead. And then, some way through the second half, just as the English begin to rest on their fat laurels, the Welsh come back with inevitable dummy-shimmying brilliance.

Taliesin has little skill but being light he can move quickly and being afraid of physical contact he has developed a keen sense of preservation which keeps him dodging. Jonathan barely has to break into a run for most of these games. Occasionally he'll put in a spurt of energy, just as Taliesin is beginning to feel patronized. Jonathan is filling out his once lissom frame, especially around the neck. Taliesin doesn't envy his brother's size. Jonathan hasn't quite yet grown into his adult body; certain parts have gone ahead of others. His nose, for instance, has outgrown his jaw and his legs are still too long. The voice has cracked into deeper octaves but it has a slightly self-conscious and pretentious bass in some of his words. The physical gap between them has widened this year and that has changed the nature of these games. If anything Jonathan has to pretend even more than usual. He can't put his weight into the tackle.

Jonathan kicks off. Taliesin's gloves fail to grip the shiny surface of the ball and he drops it in front of him.

'The referee has allowed play to continue. The English pour in on the Welsh. They're driving them back and a maul has formed.' Taliesin feels tiny as his brother envelops him, clamping gangly arms about his body and half wrestling with the ball. This close he can smell Jon's cheap aftershave and that vague bacony smell he has. They are locked like this for a while. Jonathan continues to comment as he mauls.

'Penalty. The referee has blown for a penalty. Wales failing to release the ball.'

Taliesin takes his place where the posts should be and pretends to be posts by holding up his arms, crooked at the elbow to form the two parallels. Jonathan places the ball with exaggerated precision, pulls some grass out and tosses it into the air to see where it blows. The wind is strong and lifts and sprays the grass up and out. 'And the tall figure of Jonathan Smith-Jones steps forward to take the kick.' Jonathan simulates the sound of muffled Welsh boos and English cheering and kicks the ball.

'3–0! You can't take those sort of risks with a kicker the calibre of Smith-Jones.' Jonathan does the posh accent of the English commentator. Taliesin laughs and restarts, booting the ball towards the left touch.

'It's a throw-in.' Jonathan takes the throw and Taliesin, with no one to contest the line-out but imagined Englishmen, catches it and starts to run straight for the English try line, half hearing the roar of the Welsh crowd in his head. Jonathan gives chase, dives and misses. 'A spectacular attempt.' The try line is looming . . . 'He's going to score, he must score, but what? No . . . he's dropped it, the ball has slipped from his hands. What a terrible mistake. The crowd can't believe it.' Jonathan changes accent and is immediately another commentator offering analysis. 'Well, questions must be asked about the gloves the Welsh player's wearing. Even the crowd seem to want the gloves off.' 'Gloves off, gloves off,' the crowd chants.

Gloves off, gloves off, gloves off. The crowd are right: the gloves are ruining the game, they have to come 'off, off, off.' Taliesin peels them off. The crowd rustle. He puts the gloves in his pockets and then picks up the ball only to drop it again. It hasn't slipped from his grasp, he has deliberately thrown it aside to look at his hands. He looks at them unable to believe what he doesn't see. There are no warts. Not one. Either side. All clean. They've all gone. All at a go. Perhaps they've relocated to his face. He checks, he feels, he blinks. He's never mistrusted his senses this much before. He needs separate verification.

'Look Jon!'

Jonathan squints. He wants to get on with the game. 'Well?'

'Look.' Taliesin holds out his hands as he might hold out a box of gold, frankincense or myrrh to a king.

Jonathan shrugs. 'They would have gone anyway.' He picks up the ball. But Taliesin is unable to play on. He stand there with his hands out.

'But they were all there last night. I checked them one by one. All eleven. Look!' he pleads. Jonathan spirals the ball in the palm of his hand, unimpressed. He reverts to commentary.

'The crowd begins to boo. "Get on with the game. Stop wasting time." They're slow hand clapping,' he says.

Taliesin feels bemused elation and the exasperation of not being believed. How can the evidence be so easily denied? You wait for a miracle (and this is surely a miracle – even if it has taken two days) and when it happens it's dismissed with a shrug by an unbelieving brother. It makes him want to kill the person that doubts him; he wants to strangle his brother and murder his doubt. Why doesn't Jonathan see and acknowledge the truth? Taliesin's frustration turns to evil thoughts. He's back on that island of the Flies again and his face is painted with blue woad. Jonathan is tied to the palm tree and Taliesin is dancing around him, prodding his brother in the ribs with a bamboo spear, and holding his healed hands under his nose. 'Now do you believe me?' Jonathan lifts his head and shakes it limply. Drums begin to sound . . .

'They could easily have gone in the night,' Jonathan says. 'There's nothing amazing about it.'

'They were there this morning. I checked. They must have gone while we were playing, or during breakfast. There aren't even scars,' Taliesin says.

'It's your kick,' Jonathan persists.

Can the supernatural be so unexceptional? His brother is doing his best to bring things down to earth and deny the moment its magic. He wants to get on with the game, to keep things normal and mundane. He won't extend his imagination to anything as vague and inexplicable as the sudden disappearance of eleven warts.

Taliesin touches the spot where Prime Wart was, just below the nail bed of his index finger. The skin is clear and there is no trace of anything having been there. There are a few cracks and lines, that's it.

'And the crowd have never seen anything like it. The whole

Welsh team is standing in the middle of the pitch, unable to continue. They seem to have given up. They're all looking at their hands. The referee has blown his whistle and abandoned the game. I've never seen anything like it in my life.' Jonathan punts the ball high into the late-November sky and walks away.

Miracles are amazing, until they happen. Then you have to share the news with an unbelieving world. Already the first to see the evidence has denied it. Does this invalidate the magic? Should he look for a more rational explanation in a textbook somewhere? Or is this the sign from God he's been waiting for?

It surely is. It must be a miracle. In its own way it is up there with the other miracles, the big sea-parting ones, the dead-raising ones. God has moved his little mountains. Taliesin wishes for the cameras and newsmen of the world to be there interviewing him, rolling cameras at his hands and adding reported weight to the fact. He'd like his brother and his father, everyone he knows, to flick on the news and catch this late bulletin from a small, hitherto insignificant village in Wales. 'Today in the small Welsh village of Cwmglum, God has healed the eleven warts of eleven-year-old Taliesin Jones.' Close up of hands and authoritative scientist pointing baton at the now unblemished skin. 'And here we see the totally smooth surface where only two days ago the warts clustered about the fingers. I can only say that science has no answer to this remarkable event. It is indeed a miracle.'

MEERA SYAL

Anita and Me

Like every nine-year-old girl, Meena can't wait to grow up and break free from her parents. But, as the daughter of the only Punjabi family in the mining village of Tollington, her fight for independence is different from most.

Meena wants fishfingers and chips, not just chapati and dhal; she wants an English Christmas, not the interminable Punjabi festivities she has to attend with her embarrassing Aunties and dreadful cousins, Pinky and Baby – but more than anything, more than mini-skirts, make-up and the freedom to watch *Opportunity Knocks*, Meena wants to roam the back-yards of working-class Tollington with the feisty Anita Rutter and her gang.

Written with extraordinary grace and charm, and just a hint of wistfulness, *Anita and Me* is a unique vision of a British childhood in the Sixties, a childhood caught between two cultures, each on the brink of enormous change.

Meera Syal, a British born Indian, is an actress with a number of TV, theatre and film credits, including the screenplay for the film *Bhaji on the Beach*. She has also appeared in *The Real McCoy* and *Have I Got News For You*.

APRIL   £9.99   HARDBACK

Anita and Me

MY NANIMA'S ARRIVAL did not go unnoticed in the village, probably because when papa finally returned with his precious cargo from the airport, he drove up to the house tooting his horn furiously, whereupon a noisy welcoming committee made up of mama, Auntie Shaila and Uncle Amman, Pinky and Baby, myself and Sunil, all rushed into the garden shouting and waving, causing traffic to slow down and passing women to stop and squint curiously, patting their hair into place in case there were hidden television cameras in the privet hedges.

Papa flung open the Mini door ceremoniously, and Nanima levered herself out, brushing out the creases in her beige *salwar kameez* suit with gnarled brown fingers and pulling her woollen shawl around her to ward off an imagined breeze. She had barely taken a step before mama had thrown herself into her massive bosom, laughing and crying all at once, whilst Auntie Shaila sniffled to herself as she anointed our front step with oil as a traditional gesture of welcome. (It was supposed to be coconut oil but a bottle of Mazola Deep 'N' Crispy still did the trick.)

It took at least ten minutes for Nanima to reach the front door as each of us were shoved into her path to receive a blessing from her upraised hands. I was furious that Pinky and Baby got there before me, she was not even their sodding granny and there they were in the front of the queue, collecting a few more brownie points for their next life. But I reckoned since the Collection Tin incident, I could afford to be a little generous; after all, they had not mentioned it since. Neither had they ever allowed their mother to leave them alone with me, for which I was relieved. However,

I smirked to see Nanima's confusion as she patted them on the head, and felt vindicated when I saw mama whispering their names to her, explaining, I was certain, that they were hangers-on as opposed to blood relatives.

Papa held Sunil out for inspection; his bottom lip began quivering as soon as Nanima tried to cuddle him, so she laughed instead and picked his cheek, handing him back to mama who kept up an excited monologue, 'See beta? That's your Nanima! Your Nanima has come to see you! Say Nanima! Say it!' Then I found myself looking up into my mama's face, except it was darker and more wrinkled and the eyes were rheumy and mischievous, but it was mama's face alright, and suddenly I was in the middle of a soft warm pillow which smelt of cardamom and sweet sharp sweat, and there was hot breath whispering in my ear, endearments in Punjabi which needed no translation, and the tears I was praying would come to prove I was a dutiful granddaughter, came spilling out with no effort at all.

I knew Nanima was going to be fun when she rolled backwards into the farty settee and let out a howl of laughter. As Auntie Shaila tried to haul her out, she continued laughing, shouting something to mama which turned into a loud chesty cough as she finally regained her balance. 'Meena, don't titter like that, have some respect,' papa admonished me gently. But as I handed Nanima a glass of water, one of our best glasses with the yellow and red roses around the rim, she chucked me under the chin conspiratorially and said something to papa who shook his head resignedly.

'What?' I badgered him. 'What did she say?'

'Nanima said you are a "junglie", a wild girl, uncivilised . . .' papa said. I ran around the front room whooping 'Junglee! Junglee!' and doing mock kung fu kicks at my shadow on the wall to make Nanima laugh even harder.

'Oy!' papa shouted over the din. 'It is not a compliment, you know!' But Nanima's expression told me it was exactly that.

The rest of the evening passed in a stream of constant visitors bearing gifts of sweetmeats and homemade *sabzis*, anxious to meet one of the generation they had left behind and to catch up on the latest news from the Motherland. However, those of my Uncles and Aunties seeking the latest political intrigue in Delhi or the hot filmi gossip from Bombay ended up sorely disappointed as Nanima now resided in a tiny village in the Punjab and was not exactly equipped to be India's latest Reuters' correspondent. Most of the conversations began with someone asking, 'So! Tell us the latest, Mataji . . .' Nanima then launched into a jaunty monologue, punctuated by loud slurpings of tea and surreptitious massaging of her feet which silenced the questioner into a series of polite smiling nods.

'What did she say?' I tugged on papa's sleeve.

'She said that they are building a new road in Bessian town centre and that Mrs Lal's daughter is finally getting married to a divorced army officer . . .'

'Who is Mrs Lal?' I continued.

Papa shrugged his shoulders. 'Who knows?' he whispered back, stifling a grin.

But frankly, Nanima could have answered their continuous questions with a series of burps or simply fallen asleep mid-sentence, and every gesture would have still been received with the same reverence and adoration. For her audience was there not because of what she said but because of who she was, a beloved parent, a familiar symbol in her billowing *salwar kameez* suit whose slow deliberate gestures and modest dignity reminded them of their own mothers. Of course they would deify her, their own guilt and homesickness would see to that, but how could this small vessel possibly contain the ocean of longing each of them stored in their bellies? It was only when papa lined the three of us up for a photograph, daughter, mother and grandmother, all of us the product of each other, linked like Russian dolls, that it struck me how difficult it must have been for mama to leave Nanima and how lonely she must have been. Indeed, I had never seen mama so fresh and girlish, as if some invisible yoke had been lifted from her shoulders and she regained the lithe legs and strong back she must have had when she cycled to and from college, humming the tunes my father sang to her through her shuttered bedroom window. I vowed then that I would never leave her, this wrenching of daughter from mother would never happen again.

Of course, this would not stop me having all the adult adventures I had been planning for myself; I would still travel and cure sickness and rescue orphans and star in my own television series, I would just have to make sure mama came with me, that was all. My mind drifted into practical overdrive, as it did with all my daydreams. It was never enough to have a vague picture, such as 'I save Donny Osmond from near death and win a medal'. I had to know what I was wearing, whether it was a fire in a top London hotel or a runaway horse in a summer meadow, what the weather was like, who was watching and how my hair looked at the moment of rescue.

It was an annoying trait, I admit, and often I got bored with the fantasy halfway through, bogged down by stylistic detail when I should really have been concentrating on the emotion and wish-fulfilment side of things. But I needed to calculate how feasible it might be for mama to leave her teaching job and what make of car would be large enough to contain my vast wardrobe and yet be safe enough for mama to manouver in a three-point turn. So I barely registered the click of papa's camera and in the photograph, which I still have, mama and Nanima are beaming full into the lens like similar yet not matching bookends, and I am gazing dreamily into the middle distance, as if I am barely lending my body for the pose. 'Va Meena!' papa had said when the photograph came back from the chemist's. 'You have the soulful look of a movie star!' I had not the heart to tell him I was mentally choosing my car upholstery.

Still, that evening our house seemed to vibrate with goodwill and hope, the air felt heady and rare, the food seemed mountainous and never ending, even Sunil giggled and chirruped his way through dinner from his usual position on mama's hip, trying to form passing adult words like some drunk parrot. It was such an unseasonably warm evening that every possible window was flung open as the house became more crowded and noisy, until suddenly, the front door was ajar and our guests began spilling out into the garden, still clutching their drinks and balancing plates of food. This threw me into a minor panic; Tollington front gardens were purely for display purposes, everyone knew that. And here were all my relatives using our scrubby patch of lawn like a marquee, laughing and joking and generally behaving as if they were still within the security of four soundproofed walls.

It felt so strange to hear Punjabi under the stars. It was an indoor language to me, an almost guilty secret which the Elders would only share away from prying English eyes and ears. On the street, in shops, on buses, in parks, I noticed how the volume would go up when they spoke English, telling us kids to not wander off, asking the price of something; and yet when they wanted to say something intimate, personal, about feelings as opposed to acquisitions, they switched to Punjabi and the volume became a conspiratorial whisper. 'That woman over there, her hat looks like a dead dog . . . The bastard is asking too much, let's go . . . Do you think if I burped here, anyone would hear it?'

I stood uncertainly on the front porch and watched helplessly as the Aunties and Uncles began reclaiming the Tollington night in big Indian portions, guffawing Punjabi over fences and hedges, wafting curried vegetable smells through tight-mouthed letterboxes, sprinkling notes from old Hindi movie songs over jagged rooftops, challenging the single street light on the crossroads with their twinkling jewels and brazen silks. Usually, mama and papa were the most polite and careful neighbours, always shushing me if I made too much noise down the entries, always careful to keep all windows closed during papa's musical evenings. But tonight, I noted disapprovingly, they were as noisy and hysterical as everyone else. I had never seen the Elders so expansive and unconcerned, and knew that this somehow had something to do with Nanima.

I hesitated on the porch steps, unsure whether to flee indoors, dreading what the reaction of any passers-by might be, but also strangely drawn to this unfamiliar scene where my two worlds had collided and mingled so easily. There was a whiff of defiance in the air and it smelled as sweet and as hopeful as freshly-mown grass. Nevertheless, I froze when I heard the footsteps approaching the crossroads. It was two of the Ballbearings Committee, I was not sure which ones as in their Gooin' Out Outfits of tight shiny tops and optimistically short skirts, they all looked like sisters. By the way they were holding onto each other, I could tell they were on their way home from the Mingo disco, although they seemed to sober up immediately as they caught sight of our crowded front garden. Two pairs of red eyes ringed in creased blue powder took in the teeming, laughing masses and two lipstick smudged mouths broke into wide wicked grins.

'Ay up, Mr K! Havin a bit of a do then?' one of them shouted, every word sliding into each other so it sounded like a strangely musical babble.

'Oh yes ladies!' papa called from somewhere near the hedge. 'Come and join us! Whisky, yes?'

Even in this light I could tell papa's face was flustered; he was wearing that lazy benevolent expression that always settled on his face after a good session with the Uncles, who were now gathering around him, seemingly impressed that papa was acquainted with some of the local talent.

'Whisky!' the other Ballbearings Committee member shrieked. 'Hark at him! Posh or what. Not on top of Malibu, thanks Mr K. Don't wanna be picking sick out of me birdbath again tomorrer!' The women's swooping laughter met the men's bass chuckles and it really did sound like a beautiful, improvised song, as beautiful as any of papa's free-fall scales he would perform at the harmonium. 'Yow have a good time, Mr K!' the women called to papa as they staggered off. 'The world looks better when yow'm pissed, don't it?'

We got off fairly lightly after that; if any of our neighbours did object to the din, they did not tell us. A couple of passing cars slowed down to have a good look at us, and somewhere around eleven o'clock, an old man passing on his bicycle narrowly missed clipping the public telephone booth as he caught sight of our party. But by then I had got used to it, this world within a garden, and by the time papa sidled up to me and gave me a bristly kiss laced with fumes and tobacco, I felt as if some heavy invisible cloak had fallen off my shoulders and I had grown a few feet taller. Out of nowhere, papa said, 'You really must learn Punjabi, Meena. Look how left out you feel. How will you ever understand your Nanima, huh?'

I felt wrong-footed, vulnerable. It had been such a good evening and now papa was asking me questions for which I had no instant replies.

'Leave the girl alone!' Uncle Amman called out from a dark leafy corner, his cigarette end glowing and fading like a wheezy firefly. 'Now her Nanima is here, she will learn soon enough!'

Papa patted my cheek and squeezed me tightly. 'She is my jaan, my life,' he said brokenly, and went inside for a refill.

When I finally dragged myself up the stairs after the last visitor had gone, I found Nanima sleeping in my double bed, curled up in my quilt like a cocoon. As I stood there, shivering in my nightie, mama entered quietly with Sunil sleeping in her arms. She carefully placed him in his cot at the foot of the bed, a mere gesture as he would be up in a few hours time, ready for the transfer to her bosom, and led me to the far side of my bed, motioning me to climb in. Sensing my resistance, she whispered, 'There is nowhere else for Nanima to sleep. And anyway, you are so lucky. She has the warmest tummy in the world. Get in. And don't fidget or you will wake her.'

I sidled in beside Nanima, pulling in as much quilt as I dared which barely covered my ankles and knees. She was snoring gently and breathed in huge deep sighs which seemed to swell her body to twice its size, her large stomach looked like a slowly rising loaf of bread which quickly deflated with every exhalation. Then quite suddenly she let out an enormous rasping fart which seemed to go on forever and shook the quilt around her, making me collapse into a fit of giggles which I had to stifle into my pillow. Then she heaved herself fully around so that she was facing me and dragged me under her arm where it smelt yeasty and safe, tucking the quilt around me expertly, imprisoning my freezing feet in between her soft fleshy knees. Then she opened one eye briefly and said, 'Junglee!' before dropping off to sleep.

At some point in the night I had a strange dream; Sunil was crying, nothing new in that, and I heard mama's footsteps pad into the room. Then there were two voices, mama's and Nanima's which reminded me of the wood pigeons who would coo to each other under the eaves each morning. Then Sunil began crying again, for some reason he was still in the room; and then I heard a song, or rather I felt it, a lilting lullaby in a minor key which made me think of splashing stone fountains in shadowed courtyards and peacocks ululating on tiled flat rooftops, sunlight glinting off the deep blue feathers encircling their necks. And then I saw, although my eyes were closed, I saw Nanima rocking Sunil in her arms, quite violently I thought, and rise slowly into the air and circle the room, her pyjama bottoms flapping like Hermes' wings at her ankles, whilst he laughed with delight and tried to catch the sparks fizzing from her fingertips. When I woke up the next morning, I found myself looking into a pair of muddy doggy eyes. Sunil was lying across Nanima's breast, sucking his thumb contentedly whilst she snored on, oblivious. From that day on, Sunil slept in his own cot, sometimes for eight hours at a stretch, and only a few days later, sat on papa's lap for the first time ever to eat his breakfast.

MICHELLE CHALFOUN

Roustabout

In this vibrant debut, Michelle Chalfoun brings an insider's eye for detail to the story of Mat, a tough, sassy, yet vulnerable young woman, who has been raised in the circus but is determined to break away.

Exotic, exciting, shimmering with danger and adventure, the circus is a world in which dreams can take flight and the imagination be set free. But not for Mat, who works as a roustabout in the tent crew. For her, it is a harsh demimonde of no-hopers. Theirs is a world dominated by violence, sexual exploitation, alcoholism and drug abuse. Like many, Mat must struggle every day just to survive, while in her heart she dreams of escape, of true love, of a life beyond the confining ropes of the arena. Peopled with a memorable cast of extraordinary characters – Jayson, Mat's sadistic lover and the ringcrew boss, Tattoo Lou, the multi-coloured horse trainer, Al, the cross-dressing circus cook, Tante, the fire-scarred wardrobe mistress – Mat's story is by turns tender, funny, harrowing and uplifting.

Michelle Chalfoun gave up dance studies at New York University while still in her teens to join a circus which was performing nearby. She travelled with them for three years. *Roustabout* is her first work of fiction.

MAY   £9.99   HARDBACK

Roustabout

THE TRAILER SMELLS hot and close, like sweat. We lie on the bed naked, bodies close, Jay between us. I can barely see Lou's lips move as she gives directions. Movement is slow and confused. There are many arms and legs; I keep losing track of my own. Lou motions and Jay turns me 180 degrees towards her. I become distracted by the fish swimming through her ribcage, the eagles nesting on her hip. Her hands make wide slow circles across my breasts.

Curious, clinical, I explore her. So this is how it looks, I think as I examine a pierce, a tattoo, her vagina. I note the smell (like sheets after sex), the taste (lemon and salt), texture (like an oyster). I remember the biology book a bleacher boy showed me long ago. The pictures of the segmented worm, the frog, the man and woman. Illustrated onionskin pages peeled away to reveal layers of internal organs underneath. I decide her vagina looks more like a dried pear half than an oyster.

When Jay enters Lou, I expect to be jealous, but I'm nothing. I look at this man I have fucked for over six years and wonder what this means. Then I wonder if I'm still high, but I lose that thought tracing the horses galloping across Lou's heaving back. When Jay pushes her off to finish in me, I focus on the screen door, and what lies beyond it.

In me, he says, 'Tell Lou how you like it.'

I don't understand till he raises his hand over me.

'Hard.' I mouth the word.

'Louder.' He pulls his hand back further. There is a familiar tension in his fist.

'Hard, *I like it hard!*' I scream at them both.

'Good, good,' Lou says.

Only now do I return to my body, ashamed.

Horse dress rehearsal. I limp across the ancient runways to the bigtop. Too bright morning. The sun burns through my skin to my bruised and dirty parts inside.

Bitter coke-stained mucus drips down the back of my throat, and I remember last night. I can look down on my body like looking down on a black and white photo. Jay's behind me; she's in front. I'm pinned in the middle.

Hush now, they murmur. Relax and it won't hurt so much.

They fight inside me, tearing through the thin membrane wall. They hurt me. She enjoys it, he does.

I do too.

My abdomen cramps. Sharp and swift like a cut. I kneel on the pocked tarmac, clutching my stomach. I bite the insides of my cheeks, my tongue, I bang my head with my fists.

My rigging knife presses into my left thigh. I could use it to peel off every inch of skin that enjoyed being touched last night. I could stick it up me, gut myself like a fish. Maybe, if I'm raw hollowed-out meat, I'll feel clean again.

Broken clamshells and pebbles mark my face. I'm curled on the tarmac in a fetal position. I'm going crazy. No one can find out I'm crazy. I tell myself over and over: I can control this. I can.

The ringside seats are actually quite full. Performers take up most of the center section; Ringmaster Fabrizio sits alone in a box seat. Tante hovers near the chute, hidden in the shadows of side grandstand.

Electricians perch ready on their spot platforms; the band tunes up on the bandstand. Jayson doesn't sit; he stands stiffly at the curtain, ready to pull it open. I feel like I'm the only one uninterested in this new act, this new opening for the second half. The tent looks alien to me; if Al didn't have me by my elbow, I'd run from this blue canvas cage. Instead we join Tom ringside.

The music begins, one long high note. In the middle of the gold velour curtain a white stain of light widens. The other instruments join in. Someone hidden lowers the mirrored ball from the rigging.

'Goddamn ball,' Tom whispers. Side spots hit the rotating mirrors with cool colored gels. Sharp flashes of blue and purple scatter around the tent. An appreciative murmur rises from the center section; all the performers wish their lighting was so dramatic. Blue and purple shards stab my swollen brain. Even with both hands secured around my mug, I can't raise the coffee to my lips; when I try, I shake so hard it spills over.

The music throbs in rhythm with my head, and I wonder how I'll get through this act. This day, this life.

In the ring, the curtains open slowly to reveal the white gelding. Lou steps into the ring wearing white sequined gauze. A spot picks her up, sends pink shimmers rippling through the tent. Her costume covers every tattoo, yet she doesn't look frumpy, just classy.

'Tante's outdone herself,' Tom says.

'Yeah, she's got a good eye for detail.' I wonder if Tom can smell last night on me.

Lou hits the gelding on his flank, sending him center ring, into a blinding white spot. Two gauze wings sprout from his shoulders. Covered with mirrors, they flash as brilliantly as the disco ball. Purple and blue sparks bounce off the wings as the horse shies sideways, out of the spot. He's not used to the wings' weight; or maybe the bright new lighting spooks him.

Lou's whip flicks. She hisses. The gelding freezes, and the spot catches him again. Now Lou steps regally into the ring and holds him under the light by his bridle. She styles, bows; we clap on cue.

Jay steps from the wings to receive her cape. With a flourish, she whips it off and over the gelding's head. He paws the dirt. He blows air hard through his nostrils.

She mumbles, 'Good, good.' Calming. Warning.

Jay folds her cape over his arm, bows slightly to her. She styles again; we clap again.

The music changes to an upbeat version of 'Eight Miles High.' I want to hold my hands over my ears, but I can't figure out where to put my coffee mug.

Music booming; lights flashing; the tent's heating up. I look for signs of special communication between Lou and Jay. But she concentrates on putting the white gelding through a round of solo tricks. After one chorus, Jay opens the curtains again, to let in four more horses.

These only wear headdresses of white feathers. Lou cracks her whip and they all 360 in line. The winged gelding spins in the middle. Halfway through this spin, his wings hit the eyes of the gray to his left. Tom flinches. Jay half steps toward the ring. Tante disappears under the sidewall. I drop my coffee between the floorboards.

Lou's lips move fast now, but the music carries away her commands. The frightened gray ignores her. He bites the white's wings. Her whip flicks the gray. She aims for the white. Instead of grazing his flank, her whip catches his costume.

The wings shift forward, tumble in his face.

A deep intake of collective breath.

The white gelding takes off around the ring. He runs full tilt, tries to shake off the wings. His hooves pound the ringcurb. Silently, I cheer him on.

Lou whips, shouts. He doesn't hear. He is running from those stupid wings, this stupid act. He shakes his head wildly. Feathers and sequins fly off his back. The other horses shy from his heaving costume. We sit frozen in our seats, watching Lou lose control.

The horse aims to break out. Runs for the chute, the gold curtain. The other horses step aside, give him plenty of room for escape. But Jay steps in front of the velour, blocking this exit.

He gallops past Jay. Vaults over the ringcurb and out the ring. Ringmaster Fabrizio yells Italian to Tom; Tom looks at me. The white gelding heads for the sidewall.

Tom and I run behind him now. We're afraid for the tent. Stopped short by the blue vinyl, the horse banks hard left, escapes under side grandstand.

Tom and I follow him into the steel maze that supports the seats.

Under the bleachers it's dark and close, the only light a small amount of sun filtering through gaps and pinholes in the sidewall. Blue steel beams cross in confusion, supporting floorboards and seats. Garbage nets hung between the steel stringers hold fragrant reminders of last year's season. Panicked feet thud above us.

Ahead, the horse trots around the outer ring of scaffolding. The enclosed space must frustrate him; every jerk of his head kicks a floorboard out of place. Each board knocked out reveals a rectangle of show lights; purple and blue lights escape the ring and shine down through the holes. Bright colors dance across the steel structure.

'We have to get him before he knocks the whole thing down on our heads,' Tom says quietly. The horse whinnies and kicks a stringer support. The bleachers groan.

Tom yells up through a knocked-out floorboard hole. 'Get off the bleachers, you damn fools. If he knocks out a stringer, the whole thing'll collapse.' The feet and voices move away.

We creep forward carefully. Like walking the high wire, our hands held out in front. For blindness, balance, warning, protection. I have difficulty picking through the confused darkness of this usually familiar terrain. The smell of rotted cotton candy and mildewed net mixes with horse sweat and horse fear.

'I found him,' I yell. Tom appears at my shoulder.

Actually, I heard him breathing before I saw him. He lies in a tangled heap of gauze and mirrors. His wings are wrapped around the main support of center section G, his head caught in a garbage net. His left hind leg bends at an unnatural angle, while the rest of his heaving body is wedged between the boards of the hippodrome track and the muddy ground.

'Stay and watch him,' Tom says.

'He isn't going anywhere,' I say, but Tom has already ducked under the sidewall.

Heat rises off the horse's steaming hide. He can't move, pinned as he is. I crouch closer to him, butt to heels. I look in his eyes and not at those wings. His eyes are rolled back and up, so he can see me even though he can't turn his head.

'Hey now, hey. Don't be afraid,' I say. 'Relax and it won't hurt so much.' I consider touching him, but worry that might spook him. Above our heads, people argue about what went wrong. Lou's voice filters down, blaming. The horse and I look at each other. There is talk of missed cues, foolish costuming, unrealistic expectations.

'How do you feel?' I ask the horse this only to hear my voice, as if by talking to him I do something worthwhile. He stares at me, not moving.

'Do you hurt much?' I know he does. 'Don't be afraid. It's gonna be okay. Lie still; it'll all be over soon.' I hear Tom above us now, telling Lou the situation. She tells him to go ahead, just give her a chance to get the other horses out of the tent.

His breathing slows. I tell him Tom will fix him up fine. That it wasn't his fault. The act was stupid, and it wasn't fair to spring those dumb wings on him like that. It's not like he had a choice. It's not like he could've gone home.

There's a flash of light. Tom ducks under the sidewall. My knees crack when I straighten up.

Tom also tells the horse it's going to be okay. 'Good, good,' we both murmur, like parents to a sick child. The horse doesn't struggle anymore. He's simply looking up at me, waiting till this is all over.

Tom moves me back with gentle pressure on my arm. But I watch when he raises the rifle to his shoulder. I watch Tom aim, inches from the pure white head.

I tell my future self to remember this always: The white day bleeding under the dark blue sidewall, the horse's ragged breath, Tom's smell of tobacco and diesel, the cold bead of perspiration tracking from my armpit to my waist. How the horse's eyes are wet. How they shine. How they hold mine.

Wide open, I look and listen. The moment when the trigger sticks before it engages. Last swallow, last blink. The last breath in, no chance for out. I'm looking and listening when Tom drops him. The horse shudders once, and is still.

I crouch near the horse again, butt to heels. His eyes are in the same position, rolled back and up, but the light doesn't reflect in them so well anymore. Already he has death cataracts. The hole in the middle of his forehead releases the sweet milk smell of bone and blood suddenly exposed. A fly lands on the bullet hole. It walks jerkily around the edge, tasting.

Tom rests his hand on my shoulder. 'How do you feel?'

'Fine,' I say, but I don't move. What I'm thinking is this: I've never seen the exact moment of death so close. I've seen already dead; I've seen the process of dying, but never the transition. Never the death.

I say, 'It's just interesting, you know? Like in a scientific way. Like biology.'

His hand on my other shoulder, he lifts me to my feet. 'I'm wondering if you're ready to walk out of here. You feel like you can deal with this later?' He gestures at the horse with his chin.

I have to think. There's the horse, and here I am. I wonder if I can do it later. It's my job, I figure. I'll go to the tent truck and get some spare line. I'll round up a crew and take care of this.

And tomorrow we'll break down the tent. Tomorrow we'll drive off for a new season. Another season.

There's a pain in my gut worse than before. Something I can't identify. Halfway out into the blinding day, it hits me.

I'm jealous of the horse.

SUZANNAH DUNN

Venus Flaring

Ornella and Veronica are the very best of friends, inseparable throughout the trials and minute details of their lives, sharing everything, hiding nothing. They grow up and find their way into the world together – Ornella, flamboyant and domineering, becomes a doctor, Veronica, observant and self-possessed, a journalist. But then something goes horribly wrong between them, and what was once the truest of friendships disintegrates into an obsessive nightmare of smouldering resentment that can barely be controlled. As Ornella's loyalty fades, Veronica's desperate need for reconciliation becomes a matter of life and death – and if you can't trust your best friend with your life, then who can you trust?

'Susannah Dunn is a gifted writer.'   *The Times*

Suzannah Dunn was born in 1963 and lives in Brighton. She is the prize-winning author of a novella and collected stories, and three previous novels, including *Blood Sugar* and *Past Caring*.

MAY   £9.99   HARDBACK

Venus Flaring

FOR ME, THE big surprise of Ornella's new life was that she had a car. That her father had *given her* a car. 'But what use is a car?' she despaired to me. 'What I need is a washing machine.'

This was true. I had seen the piles of clothes that she dropped on Billy's bedroom floor, elephantine droppings of clothes. But her father had given her a car because, she explained to me, he did not like to think of her travelling by tube. (Why not? For the same reason that the rest of us had lost enthusiasm for travelling by tube? Had he seen *American Werewolf in London*?) I teased her, 'And he *does* like to think of Guido travelling by tube?' Because he had not bought a car for Guido.

She shrugged. 'Maybe it's that I'm a girl.'

'Most definitely you're a girl,' I said, 'but *I'm* a girl, and no one has bought *me* a car.'

It was not, however, a car for a girl, not cheap, small, square, slow. And it was new. But her father could not buy her a licence. So she decided that Guido could have use of the car in return for lessons. And for half of the money given by her father for lessons. Under Guido's guidance, she passed her test within a few months.

I will never forget my first trip in the car with her. It is on a Sunday, when we have had a lunch finishing with chocolate bars melted and poured over ice cream. When she had melted the chocolate, Ornella had to chip the block of ice-cream from the glacier which had formed in the freezer compartment of her fridge. She was certain that the ice-cream was vanilla, but when it was excavated, we saw that it was Double Chocolate Chip. So it was a particularly heavy lunch. Now we are in the garden, sitting on kitchen chairs. Ornella leans – wobbles – from her chair to tell me, 'When I grow up, I'm going to buy a lounger.'

'When I grow up, I'm going to *be* a lounger.'

'Which neatly sums up the difference between us,' she says, and laughs.

I return to the newspapers, one of which I have bought, the others which I would never buy but have found around the house. Some of which I have already read through to The Week Ahead On Radio, others in which I have not yet even turned to the celebrity profile. Sunlight is uneven in the garden, splashed over one side of a bush, stencilled onto the wall of the house. It is sometime between one and five in the afternoon: I have no notion of the time, except that there is plenty but will have to be plenty more before I can face food again.

Ornella complains, 'I'm bored.'

'Why don't you go and do some revision?'

Turning to me, she replies, 'It's Sunday,' and then turns away again: answer enough.

But my question was genuine: I have no exams in my second year, but everyone else is busy with them. Billy is in the library and Leah has tried to revise in the garden but was distracted by the sunshine. No, she was *intoxicated* by the sunshine: flushed and unsteady, she rose from her chair after a while and returned, mumbling irritably, to the house. She had not been home for long; she had arrived even later than usual, for lunch rather than breakfast. She had announced her arrival by looking in on us in the kitchen and saying, 'I couldn't delay any longer.'

'Revision?' Ornella had called after her.

'The morning-after pill,' she had called back, from the foot of the stairs. 'Let me go and take one and then I'll come down for some coffee.'

I had quizzed Ornella, 'She *has* them, she has *more than one?*'

Spooning honey into her coffee, she had confirmed, 'She has them, she has more than one.'

Her own supply? In her bedroom?

Licking the spoon, Ornella had added, 'A legacy from Family Planning.'

The clinic, or one of Leah's boyfriends?

Ornella says, 'Let's go for a drive.'

I turn from Quotes Of The Week to look at her. She seems to have spoken to the sun.

'A Sunday drive? What are you, my grandmother?'

'Not Southend,' she says to the sun. 'Camden, or somewhere.'

'Why?' I slap shut my newspaper.

'Because I'm bored.'

I throw the paper down and bend, groaning, for a magazine.

'You're interested in Elton John's latest transplant?' She has spoken without moving her head, barely moving her lips.

I let the picture of Elton John slip from my fingers, reach hurriedly for another section of the paper. 'I have to read the reviews.'

'Oh, read them to me.'

I know that below this request lurks an iceberg of sarcasm.

'Okay,' I drop the Books section, 'I'll go and hunt for my shoes.'

'Leave them. You don't need shoes: wheels, not heels.'

So I tip-toe to the car, tip-bare-toed behind her, around the house to the car, my soles prickly with abandon.

In the car, she takes my sunglasses from my eyes.

I flinch from the swipe of sunlight. 'Ornella!'

She replies, 'I couldn't find mine.'

Speechless, I tut savagely.

And she wails, 'I can't drive in this sunshine without sunglasses.'

And I can't sit here. So I turn away from the glare. Turn inwards. To find that that I feel sick. That my innards have been hijacked by chocolate.

Several streets later, and she has said nothing more. Is she coping with the driving? I look sideways through the haze of my nausea, see nothing but my sunglasses. I need to see her eyes to know her mood. Mood rings, mood stones, they were a craze when I was a child: the colour of the stone on my finger swilling between brown, green and blue to paint a picture of my mood. A murky picture, though: what was a brown mood? And, in any case, why did I need to be shown my own mood?

I shut my eyes.

Eventually she says, 'Look at these houses,' and her words, after the silence, are surprisingly tuneful.

So I brave the glare, and look around. White houses. Familiar London-white-houses. But not totally white. Nor, on closer inspection, even mostly so. The borders of the windows and doors are white, but the walls are bare brick. The dense brickwork is worn slightly unevenly to give a grain to each wall. Yet it is the white which is striking: wood and plaster vulnerable to chipping and rot but so obviously unchipped and unrotted, so *very white*. And the windows: these are houses of windows. Houses of servants, too, originally, I suppose, to keep the windows clean. The windows are huge silvery leaves, to drink sunlight from doubtful English skies.

'This is the kind of house that I want,' Ornella says.

'Rather different from the house that you *do* have.' I like her house, her little rented house, but sometimes, looking from the end of the street or the garden, I feel depressed. Perhaps because it is an old house, has held so many lives. No, because it is no older than these houses. It is *obviously* old. In poor condition. A terraced house, for poor people. So many short lives of long moments. I turn away from this thought, switch on radio.

If I can't have you, I don't want nobody, baby . . .

This is familiar: I close my eyes and concentrate. And after a moment, I remember: *Yvonne Elliman*. Not that this means much, not that this was ever much more than a collection of sounds at the end of the record: *EevnEllimnon Cabiddle Radio.* But now I remember: this record belongs to a summer, nineteen-seventy-something. I am certain that it was summer because I remember heat and darkness, which means summer nights. And *big*: this is what comes to mind; but even though I try hard, squeeze shut my eyes, squeeze out the world, squeeze into my memory, I cannot go beyond this simple sense of *big*. Excitement? Nights out? If so, I am remembering a world that I never knew, because there was nothing *big* about my world in nineteen-seventy-something. Suddenly I have a suspicion that I am remembering *Saturday Night Fever*: was this on the soundtrack? Yes. I went to see *Saturday Night Fever* with Abi. It was X-rated, so we had to pretend to be four years older than we were. We relied on our platform shoes.

I open my eyes, ask Ornella, 'Have you seen Abi recently?' Because Abi is a student in London, too.

'Not for a couple of months.'

We have slowed alongside a shop displaying uniforms. I suppose that uniforms have to come from somewhere. Wipe-down overalls, in pastels, for domestics, auxiliaries, caterers. Pinched by those belts which are never worn except by women in uniform: the thick band of elastic with a butterfly of buckle, no loose ends, no sharp edges. No give, either: no good for pregnancy, or water retention.

'How was she?'

'Fine.' But she shrugs to retract this ringing *Fine*, backtracks to, 'Well, same as ever.'

Same as ever? 'But was her ankle still sprained?'

'Oh,' a short note of surprise, of apology, she had forgotten, 'Yes: same as ever except for the ankle.'

I saw Abi three or four months ago. *What* I saw of her when she stepped into the doorway of the pub was her hair, her *lack of* hair: it had been cut short, she had been shorn. Her ears were exposed. Tipped into the light. Tipped *with* light. And then she looked around the room for me and I saw her eyes, suddenly so big in a head of short hair. There was no smile, merely something to pass for a smile, a spasm of recognition. Then she stepped from the doorway and I saw the limp. Odd for someone who is usually so symmetrical. She came very slowly and unevenly towards me. I did not know which to mention first, the haircut or the injury. Both so drastic, so physical. Even though I knew better, I could not help but feel that the two were connected, that her hair had been cut because of her injury: lack of hair, lack of health;

operations, and infestations. When she reached me, she lowered herself carefully into a chair and sent me a little smile across the table. No, not a smile, but something to share, something which I was supposed to understand. Something like an appeal, an admission of failure, a wince of exasperation.

I puzzled, 'Your leg . . . ?'

She corrected, 'Ankle,' explained, 'a sprain.'

'How?'

'Dancing.'

Dancing? I would have loved to know more but it was clear that this was all that she wanted to say. No doubt she had had this conversation many times, and perhaps never at her own instigation.

'You should go to Bev,' I finished quickly, flip: Bev, trainee physio.

A sulky roll of her eyes, 'Bev, God, yes,' *I'd forgotten Bev*. She busied herself with a packet of cigarettes from her pocket.

As far as I knew, she was a non-smoker. I raised my eyebrows, nodded towards her busy hands.

'Well, what else is there to do?' Staccato bitterness, and a nod towards the ankle. Then she cocked the lid of the packet: *Want one?*

'No thanks,' I said, 'I've given up, I'll breathe yours.'

Which she could have taken in any of a number of ways, but which she did not take at all. Instead, she took a cigarette from the packet, and began to complain about the weather.

Now I say darkly to Ornella, 'Abi was *not happy* with that sprain.'

She turns, briefly: a flick of her hard mouth in my direction. 'Strange, because I'd love to sprain mine.'

But her sarcasm has skidded over the point: I had never seen anyone so – what? – so *thrown*? Abi was so *thrown* by her injury. She had been failing to cope with being less than perfect.

But suddenly Ornella is asking, 'Did you see her boyfriend?' the question running with intrigue.

'No, because I saw her when I was home.' And everyone knows

that Abi's boyfriends do not come home. I make sure that my boyfriends do not come home with me simply because Mum and Dad expect them to sleep on the settee. Abi's boyfriends do not go with her because they belong to universities, to cities, to other countries, to anywhere but our home town.

'Well, *I* have,' she boasts.

'And?'

'Good-looking, but he makes me uneasy.'

Interested, I turn sharply to her.

For a moment she cannot turn her attention from the road, but responds with a wrinkle of her nose, a shrug of my sunglasses. 'I don't know why.'

I tease her, 'Perhaps *you* make *him* uneasy.' As soon as this is out, I realize that it could refer to her past illicit liaison with Abi. *Which We Have Forgotten.* But I see that she has not realized, and wonder how I can snatch it back unnoticed.

But she whoops happy sarcasm, 'Oh, *yes*, because I'm *terrifying.*'

And my blood stops because I hear that she believes this. And she is so wrong. Hard little Ornella: I have seen how people's words slide off her; how she knocks their efforts back to them. I know their complaints by heart: *Can't-get-through-to-her, Don't-know-how-to-take-her.* Her lack of self-knowledge frightens me, I am frightened *for her*. No, for me, too. But why? Why should the opinions of other people matter to me? Because whatever she feels, I feel, too? But she feels nothing, she remains blissfully unaware. Perhaps, then, because I feel *for her*. I feel for them, too, for missing out on her.

There is an impatient click of her tongue, the belated click of a thought into place: 'No, it's not true,' she revises, 'that Abi was the same as ever.'

I turn again, an eye-hook of attention.

'Because she had a tattoo.'

A tattoo? L-O-V-E, H-A-T-E? *Abi* had a *tattoo*?

She is yawning.

I wait.

101

Her mouth closes on the yawn, but she continues to savour it.

'Ornella?' Strange to try to hold a conversation with the side of her face.

A sleep-sticky, 'Or so she told me.'

I realize, 'You *didn't see it?*'

The corners of her mouth turn down, flicking up an expression of weariness. 'She said that it was on her shoulder,' she stops, adds, '*blade*, shoulder*blade*,' before continuing, 'and she was wearing lots of clothes.'

'Unusually.'

Ornella laughs.

'What is the tattoo?'

Her eyebrows contract. 'What do you mean, *what is it?* It's real, if that's what you mean. Real blood and guts. Not a sticker or transfer or something.'

'No, *what's the picture?*'

'Oh.' After a moment, she decides, 'Do you know, I don't know. I think I forgot to ask. I think I was more interested in how it was done.'

'How *was* it done?'

'I don't know,' she replies, happily, stomping on the pedals, 'It was so horrible that I stopped listening after a moment or two so that I wouldn't faint.'

I squeal, 'But you're a *medic.*'

A twitch in the corner of her mouth, the momentary holding down, holding in, of the tickle which turns into her smile. 'Which means that I don't like mutilation. And that I *do* know how to stop myself fainting.'

Suddenly I remember, rush, 'I don't think I told you that I saw Davey.'

'Oh, he never comes to see *me*': pitched between a sigh and a whine.

'He didn't come to see *me*, *I* went to see *him*.' He is too busy to come away. Too busy, even, to come home for the holidays. His joint course, History and Politics, involves nearly twice as much work as a normal degree. And he directs plays. This term, Brecht. In fact, *last* term, Brecht. 'You have a car, now,' I add, accusingly. 'By car, he's an hour or so away.'

'But he's so busy,' she continues, implores, her head on one side, 'he'd have no time for his old schoolfriend . . .'

I know what she wants me to say: 'That's *not true*.'

'How *was* he?' The wheedling is over; she is perky. 'How *was* the darling boy?'

'Fine.'

In fact, he had a heavy cold, a temporary blight. The lining of his face was scarlet: his nostrils and the rims of his eyes. His pallor could never hide a cold. He blooms a cold. But his indisposition gave him a cheerful air: he should have been in bed; by being up and out all day, he was daring. He survived the day with the help of the appropriate props: in the street, a big scarf wound around his neck, mouth, ears; and then, in the cafe, he had lozenges, opaque amber pebbles which he popped from a taut skin of clinical silver foil. At all times in the café he held one of these precious gems in his mouth, its presence betrayed by an occasional clink when his tongue turned it against his teeth. We spent the afternoon over a series of teapots, bathing our faces in their rust-smelling steam. Tales of his travels seeped into our conversation: strange that they came so naturally and so vividly, these tales of the equator, as rain slid down the windows.

I tell Ornella, 'I wish he'd write something about his travels.'

'Noooo,' she derides, 'Davey's not a writer. He's a chat show host, that's what he is.'

I laugh, 'He talks too much to be a chat show host.' And this reminds me, 'I'm worried, because he was talking about giving up, dropping out,' I will not say his words, which were *Getting on with it*, 'Trying for drama school instead.'

'So?' A flash of the sunglasses in my direction. 'What's wrong with that?'

Inside me, a hiss of impatience, infuriation. Because lately she has been playing devil's advocate too often. 'Well, why give up

103

anything? If he stays, he can drama himself silly and still have a degree.'

'But he's not going to *use* the degree.' Said cheerfully. A few words thrown off. Neither here nor there, to her.

'You never know,' I counter.

Her gaze leaves the road to turn to me. 'Davey? A civil servant? A teacher?' Just as suddenly, she drops me and picks up the road where she left off. 'Be realistic, Veronica.'

Me? But this is no devil's advocacy: she means what she said. But why will Davey never be a civil servant or a teacher? His choice, or the choice of others? Where is she, in this? With him, or against? Championing him, or writing him off?

She is saying from the corner of her mouth, 'Did I tell you that I'm on course to fail anatomy?'

I am surprised. 'Are you?'

No reply. Merely a twist of her mouth, empty of words, sour.

'What will happen?' *To you.*

'I'll be okay,' she says to the windscreen.

Meaning what? That she will pass? Or that if she fails, it does not matter? I realize how little I know about medics, their courses, their exams.

She turns to me with a smile, 'Don't worry,' turns back the smile, to herself, 'I'll have my big house, eventually; I won't be put off by a bit of anatomy.'

The house, these houses, I had forgotten the houses. Momentarily we have lost them because we are beneath the arch of a bridge. Similar brickwork, though: dense and dark. How do square bricks build a curve? As it arcs over us, I think I can see how the bridge is built, how it stands up, I think I can see how the bricks hold together. Their tiny straight edges and sharp angles are swept up into the huge curve. Hard-and-fast. Wedged so close that there is nowhere to move. Bricked up.

In the open air again, I wonder aloud, 'Where are we?' I look to Ornella, but her face is as blank and tough as the windscreen. 'Do you know where we are?' Merely conversational.

She says, 'London.'

Ha ha. 'Are you lost?'

Her lips move: 'I can't be lost unless I'm aiming for somewhere.'

Quite an impressive reply, putting me in my place. Or not quite. Because I begin to feel uneasy. Hoodwinked. On her blacked-out eyes, one more terrace of houses turns into a train. 'Okay, then: you're not lost, but do you know where we are?'

The lips open a while before the words: 'Trust me.'

Implying that she is doing something untrustworthy. I insist, 'And we *are* going somewhere, we're going *back*. So, do you know the way back?'

The car in front of us slows and stops but Ornella is late and heavy on the brake. Her mouth slacks into a smile as she turns to taunt, 'Do *you* want to drive?'

She knows the answer. And, 'I didn't even want to come for a drive.'

FAY WELDON

Splitting

Sir Edwin Rice has decided to divorce Lady Angelica, ex-rock star. She has behaved intolerably. He petitions the Court to set him free. Angelica fights back. She is not what he thinks – but then what woman ever is? Angelica takes a job as secretary to her husband's divorce solicitor – only to find one false personality leading to another. How is she to find herself: amongst good wife Angelica, Angel the tart, Jelly the secretary, all-male Ajax, Angela the hopeless – and only one body, albeit a beautiful one, to go round between the lot of them?

'*Splitting* is a shout of triumph about a woman who does more than survive.'

Observer

Fay Weldon was born in England and raised in New Zealand. Her work is translated into most world languages: she lives in London.

MAY   £5.99   PAPERBACK

Splitting

THERE WAS TRAUMA IN THE AIR.
Sir Edwin Rice has decided to divorce Lady Angelica Rice. Sir Edwin alleges in his affidavit to the Court – a document which the lawyer Brian Moss was now dictating to his secretary Jelly White – that Lady Angelica has behaved intolerably. And would the Court therefore put the couple asunder.

Jelly White's hand trembled.

Angelica, claimed Sir Edwin, committed adultery with one Lambert Plaidy; being discovered in flagrante delicto by Sir Edwin, and in the Rice family four-poster bed. This behaviour, typical of much similar behaviour on the part of Angelica Rice, was unreasonable and intolerable to Sir Edwin.

Yes, it was intolerable for Edwin Rice to live with Angelica Rice: his health, his happiness was at risk.

The Petitioner claimed that his spouse had acted in various other ways unacceptable to him: that she had been abusive and violent, pinching him while he brushed his teeth and otherwise molesting him; he alleged that her kissing of the family dogs amounted to bestiality, and her embracing of female guests to lesbianism. He petitioned the Court to let him go free of her.

Brian Moss heard Jelly White take in a breath of outrage between her teeth, and looked at his secretary sharply, but her face remained unmoved and her hand was steady again as it continued to race across the sheet. He went on dictating.

The Petitioner claimed that Lady Angelica made excessive sexual demands on him; that she refused to have children; that she had dirty habits; that she was drunken, and took drugs; that she failed to provide proper food for his guests, thus humiliating him. And that, all in all, her behaviour has been intolerable and unreasonable, and he wanted a divorce. Now.

'Goodness me!' said Jelly White, looking up from her shorthand pad. 'Did you write this for Sir Edwin? Doesn't it smack of overkill?'

'How well you put it,' said Brian Moss. 'But overkill is our stock-in-trade. It's our trademark here at Catterwall & Moss. We like to offer the Court offences in all available categories of unreasonable matrimonial behaviour. Offer the minimum, as too many firms do to avoid unnecessary trauma, and you risk the Court's rejection of the petition. What pretty white fingers you have!' And his strong brown fingers slid over her pale, slim ones, and Jelly White let them stay. Brian Moss did not, in any case, interfere with her right hand, only with the left, which was not observably making him money.

'Lady Rice sounds a dreadful wife for any man to have,' remarked Jelly.

'The Court will certainly believe so,' said Brian Moss. 'As it happened, I did have some trouble finding an example of physical assault. We had to make do with the bottom pinching.'

'But Sir Edwin was happy enough to allege it?' enquired Jelly, as if idly.

'Certainly,' said Brian Moss. 'With a little help from the new lady in his life.'

And he told his secretary how once, in the days before her employment, Sir Edwin had brought Lady Anthea Box along to an appointment: not the kind of thing Brian Moss usually approved of but, as it turned out, her presence had been useful. Anthea had spoken for Sir Edwin, who was not as coherent or determined as she. Bestiality, still one of the major and useful categories of matrimonial offence, had been quite a problem until Anthea reminded Sir Edwin how he had never liked the way his wife kissed the dogs.

'Perhaps he was just nervous of his wife catching something,' suggested Jelly White. 'Perhaps the fear was to do with hygiene, not sexual rivalry?'

'Country men seldom worry about things like that,' said Brian Moss, brushing the suggestion away. 'I hope you can get this document in the post today.'

'Of course,' said Jelly White, but it was two days before she did, and even then she put the wrong postal code on the envelope, so it was four days before the document reached Barney Evans, solicitor to Lady Rice. In the meantime Lady Rice had presented her own petition. She 'got in first', thus giving herself some minor advantage in the game that is divorce. The Rice couple, as Brian Moss observed, were not the kind to wait peaceably for a 'no fault, no blame' arrangement. Fault there was, blame there was, and fault and blame they'd have.

Jelly White was, as it happened, Lady Angelica Rice in disguise – or, to be more precise, in her alter ego. It was only lately that Lady Rice had begun to fear that the voices in her head had separate and distinct personalities. Dress up as Jelly White, and Jelly White, to some degree or another, owned her. All Lady Rice could do was whisper in Jelly's ear. They shared the ear, but Jelly it was who turned the head. It was unnerving.

Lady Rice concluded that she was suffering from a perforated personality: worse, that if any further trauma occurred, she would develop a full-blown split personality: she would become a clinical case. Lady Rice tried to maintain a calm attitude, and not to blow

up more storms than were unnecessary, which was why she allowed
Jelly to allow Brian Moss to fondle her and made no protest. She
preserved herself for worse emergencies, and in any case, she might
not be heard. Jelly was a strong and wilful personality.

In her petition for divorce, Lady Angelica Rice alleged adultery
between Anthea Box and her husband over a six-month period
previous to the date on which she, Lady Rice, had left the matrimonial home.

Lady Rice claimed physical assault, over-frequent and perverted
sexual activity; drunkenness, drug-taking and financial irrespon-
sibility; she asserted that her husband's relationship with his dogs
was of a sexual nature. That she had been eased out of her home,
Rice Court, to make way for Sir Edwin's paramour, Lady Anthea
Box. Lady Rice, on the other hand, had throughout the marriage
been a good and faithful wife.
Sir Edwin had behaved intolerably and she wanted this reflected
in any property settlement.

'An out-of-London court!' exclaimed Brian Moss, this seeming
to be the part of Barney Evans' letter-plus-enclosures which most
affected him. 'What a nightmare! I have no influence whatsoever
in the provinces. A nod in London is simply not as good as a wink
anywhere else. How ever are we to get this case settled? And
how strange: the wife has claimed almost the same unreasonable
behaviour as has the husband.'
'I expect it's because they were married so long,' said Jelly. 'They
can read each other's minds.'
'Eleven years isn't a long marriage,' said Brian Moss. 'There was
a couple in here the other day in their nineties wanting a divorce
by consent. I asked them why they'd left it so long and they said
they'd been waiting for the children to die.'

He laughed; a deep, hoarse, unexpected laugh at a pitch which made the many racing prints on the wall rattle, and Jelly laughed too, at his joke. Her tinkly little laugh made nothing rattle, but he pinched the swell of her bosom where it disappeared under her blouse. Just a little pinch: friendly. She had taken off her white woollen sweater. It was a hot day.

Outside the elegant Regency windows, London's traffic flowed, or tried to flow. Only emergency vehicles seemed able to make progress – police, fire, ambulance. Their sirens approached, passed, faded, with enviable speed.

'I make a good living,' observed Brian Moss, 'out of other people's need to be in the right; they like to claim the privilege of being the victim. Who's at fault in the Rice debacle is of no importance. The property is all that matters, and we'll make sure she doesn't get her greedy little fingers on too much of that. Clients assume that conduct during marriage will have an effect on a property settlement and veer it in the direction of natural justice, but it's rash to make any such assumption. Or only in the most extreme cases.'

'You don't see the Rice divorce as extreme, then? Merely run-of-the-mill?' enquired Jelly.

'Very much run-of-the-mill,' said Brian Moss, 'other than that both parties do have to go to considerable lengths to hide their income.'

And he explained that Lady Rice was once a pop star and no doubt had large undisclosed sums put away. And as for Sir Edwin, his accountants had naturally been working overtime, losing their client's assets in the books – fortunately for Sir Edwin the Rice Estate had books of enormous and wonderful complexity.

'I imagine they are,' said Jelly.

'Otherwise,' said Brian Moss, 'it's just a normal divorce. Both parties vie for the moral high ground, never noticing that a major landslip has already carried the whole mountain away. And both parties enrich me, thank God, by arguing.'

'You are a very poetic kind of man,' said Jelly White. Some of her hair had fallen free of her headband. Brian Moss caught up a strand or so between his fingers and tugged, and Jelly White smiled obligingly. Lady Rice sighed.

Thus Lady Angelica Rice had once smiled at Sir Edwin, her husband. Only now she smiled with measured guile, not an overflow of innocence. Trust and amiability had done Angelica Rice no good at all. She understood now that the transparency of innocence protected no one. She learned fast.

Lady Rice had a problem with lies and cunning. Jelly White had no such problem: they were intrinsic to her persona. Angelica had a story to tell.

*   *   *

I was married to Edwin for eleven years, and the Velcro that's marriage got well and truly stuck. The stuff is the devil to wrest apart: it can rip and tear if your efforts are too strenuous. The cheap little sticky fibres do their work well. 'Overuse', they say, weakens Velcro. If 'overused' – a strange concept: should you fasten only so often? – is there some moral implication here? – you can hardly get Velcro to stick at all. But I was not overused in the beginning. On the contrary. When Edwin and I married, when I stopped being Angelica White and became Lady Rice, I was seventeen and a virgin, though no one would have known it. Chastity is not usually associated with leathers, studs, boots, crops, whips and the more extreme edges of the pop scene which I then frequented. But my velcroing capacity to be at one with the man I loved, in spite of appearances, was pristine, firm, ready for service.

Velcro hot off the loom. I 'waited' for marriage. Extraordinary!

Edwin and I have now been apart for some months: he stayed in the matrimonial home; I left in disgrace and disarray. When it became apparent that I was in danger of having nothing whatsoever to show for my eleven years of marriage – not love, nor property, nor children, not even friends I could endure – I reckoned I had better get as near the legal horse's mouth as possible, to retrieve what I could of property and reputation; that horse being Brian Moss, and a fine upstanding ungelded beast he is, at that. Barney Evans, my own solicitor, is rather like a pit pony; forever squidging up his poor dim eyes in the sudden glare of his opponent's intellect. See me, Angelica Rice, as a bareback rider: high-heeled, fishnet-stockinged, wasp-waisted, leaping from saddle to saddle as the two blinkered legal steeds run round and round their circus ring. Jelly White running after with a bucket and spade, shovelling up the shit.

On a good night, tucked up in my high, soft bed at The Claremont, a stone's throw from Claridges, with its pure white, real linen sheets, I see myself as an avenging angel. Then I laugh aloud at my own audacity and admire myself. Fancy getting a job with your husband's lawyer's firm! On a bad night, when the fine fabric of the pillows is so wet with my tears that the down within gets dark, matted and uncomfortable, when I feel tossed about in a sea of dejection, bafflement, loss – a sea that keeps me buoyant, mind you, made extra salty by my own grief – why, then I know I am just any other abandoned and rejected woman, half-mad, worthy of nothing. Then I see that taking a job at Catterwall & Moss, in the heart of the enemy camp, is mere folly, presumption and insanity, and not in the least dashing, or clever or funny. And I worry dreadfully in case I'm found out. My moods are so extreme I feel I am two people. How is it possible to contain both in the same body?

Yet apparently it is. At least three of me look out of my two eyes.

115

Lady Rice, Angelica and Jelly: Lady Rice and Angelica fight it out for ascendency: Jelly is Angelica's creature.

Lady Rice is a poor, passive creature in my, Angelica's, opinion. That's what marriage made of her, once it began to go wrong. She'd lie about in The Claremont suffering all day if I let her. She wouldn't even bother to answer Barney Evans' letters. I, Angelica, am the one who has to get her to work each day, dress her up as Jelly White, take her to the gym, keep her on a diet, stop her smoking. I am, I like to think, the original, pre-married persona. Why she maintains she's the dominant personality round here I can't imagine. Perhaps it's because she has a title: perhaps it's because she can't face the small-town girl that's me, which is part of her and always will be.

BARBARA GOWDY

Mister Sandman

Barbara Gowdy is one of the most distinctive voices in contemporary fiction. *Mister Sandman*, her third novel, introduces the Canarys, a family quite unlike any other. Little Joan is exquisite, tiny, mute, plays the piano like Mozart and lives in a closet. Her sister Marcy is a nymphomaniac, while Sonja is enormous, earns a fortune clipping hairgrips onto cardboard and knits compulsively. Their parents, Doris and Gordon, by comparison seem quite normal, but then they keep their own peculiar habits secret for as long as they possibly can . . .

'She writes like an angel'   CAROL SHIELDS

Barbara Gowdy lives in Canada. Her short story collection, *We So Seldom Look on Love*, and two previous novels have been published to great critical acclaim.

MAY   £8.99   PAPERBACK

Mister Sandman

JOAN WAS BORN on Friday, November thirtieth, 1956, at around one-thirty p.m. Pacific time in the basement guest room of Dearness Old Folks' Home. The same room that, two years earlier, a seventy-year-old woman named Alice Gunn wrote backwards in the window grime ROT IN HELL then choked herself to death with her rubber restraining belt.

'Callous Alice' the newspapers called her in their features about Joan, because that old tragedy was dredged up and tied in to the reincarnation story. A week after Joan's birth, by which time both Doris and Sonja thought it was safe to leave her on her own for a few minutes, a reporter sneaked into the room and took her picture and then drove to White Rock and showed the snapshot to Alice's ninety-seven-year-old mother, who after Alice's death had changed old folks' homes.

'That's Ali, all right,' Alice's mother was quoted as saying. 'I'd know those bug eyes anywhere.' She said, 'Tell her new mother I'm still paying monthly instalments on the headstone, if she'd care to pitch in.'

Not just Doris and Sonja but everyone at Dearness took exception to the bug-eyes crack. Everyone at Dearness was bowled over by Joan's beauty, even the old men were. Men who found the soup-spoons too heavy asked to hold her. One man believed that Joan was the reincarnation of his first wife, Lila, who in a recent seance had talked of returning to earth for 'another go-round.' When Joan started making that odd clicking sound she sometimes did, he said, 'Yep, hear that? Those are her teeth, those are her new uppers,' resting his case. 'Well, Lila!' he said, propping Joan

119

astride his scrawny knee, 'I took the nervous breakdown, expect you heard.'

Even Aunt Mildred was under Joan's spell, and she was the one who'd predicted that Joan would be a midget or a dwarf, 'something deformed and bunched-up like' because of the tucked-in, round-shouldered way Sonja had carried herself when she was pregnant.

Aunt Mildred had gone downhill a lot further than Doris had realized. On the phone back in June she'd said come on out, failing to mention not only her throat cancer but also that she had lost her house to creditors and was moving into an old folks' home just a week before Doris and Sonja were due to arrive.

'For crying out loud, why didn't you tell us?' Doris said when they finally located her after a morning of taking taxis all over Vancouver.

'Give me the name again?' Aunt Mildred rasped.

'Doris! Gordon's wife!'

Aunt Mildred shook her head. 'Doesn't ring a bell, honey.'

Doris decided they might as well stay at Dearness anyway, might as well move into the basement guest apartment for the time being since it was dirt cheap and included meals. She booked it for the maximum allowable duration of two weeks, signing in both herself and Sonja under fake last names (and when the reincarnation story hit the headlines was she glad she had!). That same day she found a cottage for them to live in when the two weeks were up, but four days before they were supposed to go there she fell in love with a nurse named Harmony La Londe. Unhinged by this voodoo rapture and by the thought of Harmony being out of her sight for more than a few hours, she staged a little drama in Dearness's office. She pretended to telephone Gordon, then over the dial tone pretended to be hearing that he had been fired from his job and there would be no money for her and Sonja's return train fare, not for many months. She hung up slowly. She sat there blinking, one hand over her mouth. She allowed the woman who owned Dearness to pry the news out of her and she said, with dignity, 'I'm very grateful,' when the woman said, 'You and your daughter stay right here for as long as you need to.'

* * *

'You are a liar,' Harmony La Londe said upon hearing this story. She sounded nothing but charmed. She found Doris exotic, if you can believe it. When all she knew about Doris was that Doris was a housewife from Toronto who had tried to swing on the hot-water pipes, she said, 'Are you exotic or what?' This from a lesbian Negro career woman who wore see-through negligées and had painted her apartment to match her parrot.

On the ceiling of the basement corridor the water pipes were runged like monkey bars, and early one morning when Doris was on her way to the lounge for coffee she saw that a ladder had been left propped against the wall next to the stairwell. Out of pure high energy and without thinking, she climbed the ladder and reached for the nearest pipe. Harmony heard the yelp. 'Are you all right?' she called from her door.

'I had a little accident!' Doris said, scuttling down the ladder.

Harmony hurried toward her. She was wearing a red chiffon negligée, she looked on fire. Doris extended her hand and there were two pink slashes – one across her fingers, one across her palm. 'Better get that under cold water,' Harmony said.

As Dearness's head nurse, Harmony lived rent free in what had once been a second guest apartment. Doris followed her down the hall. 'Ow, ow,' she said, graduating to 'Wow' when she walked through Harmony's door. The layout was the same as Doris and Sonja's apartment but the walls were painted a brilliant lime green, and instead of venetian blinds there were drapes, orange with a black dust-web pattern. In the centre of the room, in a glittery cage that hung like a chandelier from the ceiling, a parrot squawked and flapped around.

'That's Giselle,' Harmony said. 'She's the jealous type.'

The bathroom was sunny yellow. Harmony turned on the tap

and took hold of Doris's wrist to direct her hand under the water. As if Doris were a child. No, as if she were an old lady, Doris realized. But Harmony was the older one here. In her short, slicked-back hair (Doris presumed she'd had it straightened) were single white strands like cracks. Not a line on her face, but ancient eyes and furrowed bony hands that made Doris's plump white hands look like they belonged to a lady of leisure.

'That better?' Harmony asked.

'I'll say. Listen, I hope I didn't wake you.'

'Oh, no, no, it's my day off. I was just lounging around.' She turned off the tap, then dabbed Doris's hand with the corner of an orange towel. 'What were you doing, anyway?'

Doris told her.

Harmony laughed. 'You crazy?'

'Sometimes I wonder.'

'You really wanted to swing on the pipes?' She had stepped out into the hall and opened the closet there. Doris saw shelves crammed with bottles and vials, medicines, bandages.

'Good thing I didn't, eh?' Doris said. 'I'd have brought down the whole plumbing system.'

Harmony took a tube of salve from the back of one of the shelves. 'Mrs. –'

'Oh, call me Doris.'

'Doris.' She turned and planted a fist on her hip. 'Are you exotic, or what?'

'*Me?*'

Doris wasn't aware that she had been avoiding glancing at the negligée until she glanced at it. She only wanted to give it an exaggerated once-over, as if to say, You're the exotic one around here! But the light coming from the living room had made the chiffon transparent, and so what Doris found herself looking at was her first naked woman. The high, conical breasts, the darkness of the nipples, the darkness at the crotch and the long thighs pouring down. She stared, all right. For how long? ('Long enough,' Harmony said later.) Say, fifteen seconds. Dead seconds, so evacuated of everything except for Harmony's body that staring seemed natural to Doris, a serenely clinical act, a polite one even, until the bird started squawking, 'Giselle! Giselle!'

'Yes, you,' Harmony said then. Quietly. She stepped back into the bathroom and took hold of Doris's wrist again to apply the salve.

'God, God, God,' Doris thought. She felt faint from embarrassment. Her vision blurred. Now what? Don't tell her she was going to cry!

'There you go,' Harmony said.

Doris whispered, 'Thanks.' Okay, it was over.

No, it wasn't. Harmony still held her wrist. Doris looked at both their hands, hers the most helpless thing she had ever seen. She watched Harmony lift it like food to her mouth.

'A kiss to make it better,' Harmony said before her lips touched down.

*　　*　　*

Five months later, ten days late, Sonja's water broke. It was Friday, early afternoon, and the Jolly Kitchenaires – the little band of wheelchair-bound ladies who met after lunch in the dining room to bang cutlery on cookware and belt out show tunes – were working on 'I'm Just a Girl Who Can't Say No.' You could hear them all the way down in the basement, that's how loud they were. Happily, languidly, Sonja was pencilling loops in a notebook, eating licorice Allsorts and trying to balance her grammar book on her head while, sitting next to her at the card table, her starry-eyed little tutor, Miss Florence Butson, cooed encouragement. (It turns out that a retired teacher of penmanship and deportment isn't the same thing as a retired teacher of English after all, but at a nursing home you take what you can get in the way of tutors was how Sonja and Doris were looking at it.)

Doris wasn't in the apartment that afternoon. She was hardly ever there, being too full of pep to just sit, she said, and when she did fly in, by then Sonja was usually asleep. But Sonja was often awakened by her mother's hands on her belly. First thing in the morning Doris would go for Sonja's belly again, feeling for the feet and hands, listening to the heartbeat through Sonja's navel. In her sleep she sometimes moaned, 'Baby . . . baby,' and Sonja pressed her mother's hand against herself and said, 'Right here, Mommy. Feel, Mommy.'

Nobody had prepared Sonja for her water breaking, so when she felt the sudden pressure she thought she was dying to go to the bathroom. She came to her feet, forgetting about the book, which slid off her head and onto the floor, right under the downpour.

'Oh, my,' said Miss Butson and scraped back her chair.

Sonja waddled in the direction of the bathroom. Halfway there a knifing pain bowed her backwards and she fell hard on her rear end, bringing a table and lamp crashing down with her.

'When a person tries to kiss a girl!' shrilled the Jolly Kitchenaires.

Another pain. Another. Unaccustomed as she was to pain, Sonja wasn't a good screamer and could manage only a few broken whinnies.

'I'm going for a nurse,' Miss Butson said, scurrying for the door as it opened and 'I can't be prissy and quaint!' blared in together with Aunt Mildred.

'What's all the racket?' Aunt Mildred rasped.

'She just fell right over!' Miss Butson said at a hysterical pitch.

'I want my mommy,' Sonja whimpered.

'Is she having it?' Aunt Mildred got down on her knees, joints cracking like popcorn. 'Let's take a look-see,' she said, throwing up Sonja's soaking dress and peering in. 'Huh,' she said.

'What?' cried Miss Butson.

'Get up,' Aunt Mildred ordered Sonja.

Another pain. During its long trajectory Aunt Mildred moved behind her and hooked her under the arms. 'Well, don't just stand there like a nitwit,' she rasped at Miss Butson.

Miss Butson clutched Sonja's hands and tugged, her sweet,

milky eyes ogling Sonja with an expression of terror-stricken reassurance. Sonja was no help. Between pains she felt numb from the neck down. She felt like a tiny, melting snowman's head. 'Whut you goin' to do when a feller gits flirty?' shrieked the Kitchenaires. Finally Aunt Mildred growled at Miss Butson to get out of the way, then mustering astonishing strength managed to heave Sonja onto the high four-poster bed.

'Now then,' she wheezed.

'Is it the baby?' Miss Butson asked, tremulous.

With one quavering hand Aunt Mildred fumbled at her cardigan pocket while regarding Sonja under half-closed, leathery eyelids. She pawed out a cigarette and a book of matches. When she had the cigarette lit she took a deep drag, lips puckering like a draw-string purse. 'I'll tell you what you do with left-over mashed potatoes,' she said to Miss Butson.

Miss Butson made a whimpering sound.

'What you do is –' She frowned at Miss Butson. 'What is it again?'

The next pain produced a dozen little pains that flew like sparks. 'Better get her drawers off,' Aunt Mildred said. Sonja felt hands scrambling on her belly, and then her underpants being jerked down her legs. The caressing coils of vein and the crib-like little bones, the cosy pink-and-white chamber she had envisioned her baby living in she now envisioned being scraped away by the slow, sinking rotation of a cement-block thing. 'Make way,' her aunt said, and Sonja felt her mouth opening wider and wider as if obeying or as if pantomiming her other end, but the cry skidded in her throat.

'It's out.'

'Oh, my.'

'What do you know about that, it just jumped right out.'

'Oh, my.'

'You got a hold of it there, Flo?'

'Yes, yes I think so . . .'

'Let me see,' Sonja murmured.

'It's a girl.'
'You've got yourself a girl, honey.'
'Let me see,' Sonja said.
'She's not breathing!'
'You've got to smack her.'
'Please,' Sonja said.
'Go on, Flo, really whack her one.'
'I can't . . .'
'Give her here.'
'Mind your cigarette.'
A loud slap, a faint bleat . . .
Then . . .
'FLO! FLO! SHE'S INSANE!'
Or was it, 'OH! NO! NOT AGAIN!'
Whichever, that famous, disputed scream was loud. Even the Jolly Kitchenaires heard what they agreed among themselves sounded like bad news in the hot-water pipes, likely a rupture.

*   *   *

Write off that ear-splitting cry as something mechanical or as a hysterical, multiple hallucination and you still have the mystery of why a head-first fall onto the floor didn't kill her let alone cave in or crack her skull. The only visible injury was a bruise to the left of her soft spot, a mauve quarter-sized circle from which radiated a wavy starburst of hair-thin veins so that you had to wonder (or at least Sonja did) if the bruise wasn't transmitting urgent bulletins from the afterlife.

There was the mystery of Doris calling her Joan, being inspired to call her this the first time she held her in her arms although Anne was the name that she and Gordon and Sonja had agreed on for a girl. Not until almost three years later, when Gordon looked up from his crossword puzzle and said, '*Sonja* is an anagram of *Joan's*,' did anybody realize that Doris had unwittingly branded her with her real maternity.

Her beauty was a kind of mystery, not just because it was genetically inexplicable but because it was so seductive. People always say, What a beautiful baby! but here was a baby who inspired adoration even in the blind. At Dearness the blind faltered their hands over her face and limbs and like everyone else compared her to the disadvantage of all other babies, including their own. The picture of her that the photographer took to show Callous Alice's mother also appeared in three Vancouver newspapers and generated hundreds of claims that she was the reincarnation of this or that beloved relative, pleas and orders to hand her over.

The newspapers were notified by Aunt Mildred, another curiosity when you consider that her hip broke when she fainted and she had to climb two flights of stairs to get to a phone. Fortunately, by the time the first two reporters showed up, Doris had everything more or less under control. No pictures, she said, no disturbing the mother or the baby, but as she couldn't put a lid on Aunt Mildred, let alone the other residents, all of whom were declaring they'd heard something mighty eerie, she left it to them to answer the reporters' questions. Nothing to worry about there. Thanks to her, everyone in the home was under the impression that Sonja's last name was Gorman, that she was nineteen, and that she was the bride of a doctor who had been sent to the British Honduras as part of a U.N. relief effort.

Until the to-do died down, Sonja and the baby should stay put in the guest apartment, Doris decided. She brought them their meals and otherwise took over, and it didn't occur to Sonja to feel anything aside from off the hook. The ache she sometimes felt watching her mother give Joan her bottle she thought was her womb shrinking. 'There it goes again,' she'd think and feel a reverential affection for the complicated workings of her body. When Joan's whimpers made her breasts leak she went into the bathroom to squeeze the milk into the sink. Formula was better for babies, her mother said, which was just as well in Sonja's view. She couldn't imagine her breasts being sucked by an innocent baby, especially a baby who was supposed to be her sister. Who, for that matter, might still be Callous Alice, although most of the old people who had been willing to entertain that notion had changed their minds. With a few exceptions they now called Joan Joan.

Everybody bore gifts. Lots of knitwear and blankets, a red and orange hand-quilted blanket from the Negro nurse, which Sonja thought was a bit loud for a baby but which Doris went into raptures over. Some of the residents brought money. One old couple, old pals of Alice's, showed up with a Black Velvet Chocolates box containing twenty-five silver dollars. This couple was one of the few exceptions. 'Cold, hard cash, Ali!' the man said with a wink at Joan, and then he started pestering her with questions about the hereafter. 'Blink once for yes,' he said.

'It's her huge eyes,' Doris said one night after the visitors had gone. *Jeepers, creepers, where'd you get those peepers?* she sang, venting the song in her mind. She cleared her throat (and Joan made a similar sound, imitating Doris, you'd swear) and said, 'The way they seem to see right through you.'

'Maybe they do see right through you,' Sonja said. Leaning over her mother's arm, she lightly touched a finger to Joan's bruise, a thing she did from time to time in case she picked up a message. 'Ali?' she called softly.

'Cut it out!' Doris said, and then cooed, 'Sorry' because Joan had flinched. Turning back to Sonja she whispered, 'I've had it up to here with that mumbo jumbo.'

And she meant it, even though she herself couldn't shake the feeling that there was something going on with this kid. A few crossed wires from the fall. She'd had two babies, she knew the score. A newborn shouldn't be able to focus on you the way Joan did, right across the room, it wasn't supposed to follow you with its eyes like that. Then there was her extreme sensitivity to light and noise, and all those unbaby-like sounds she came out with. The throat-clearing, the droning, the clicking, hissing.

PATRICK GALE

Dangerous Pleasures

Patrick Gale is the acclaimed author of seven novels, including *The Facts of Life*, of which Armistead Maupin said, 'This is a monumental feat of imagination, achingly true and beautiful.' In *Dangerous Pleasures*, Gale's most brilliant pieces of short fiction are collected together for the first time.

His subjects are wide-ranging and various – curious childhood loyalties, long-hidden memories, newly discovered joys, startling secrets, dislocated relationships, overwhelming, thrilling passions. In prose that is always vivid and fresh, Patrick Gale explores the subtle boundaries that shift between the fantastic and the shockingly real. With characteristic insight and wit and with consummate ease, he draws the reader into lives both familiar and strange, revealing a world that shines with possibilities and will never fail to delight.

Patrick Gale was born in 1962 on the Isle of Wight. He was educated at Winchester and Oxford, and now divides his time between London and north Cornwall. He is the author of seven novels, including *The Facts of Life, Little Bits of Baby, The Cat Sanctuary* and *Kansas in August*.

JUNE   £9.99   HARDBACK

Dangerous Pleasures

THE BREATH WAS now coming so slowly from Shuna's mouth that Shirley found herself beginning to count in between each painful, creaking exhalation.

'Not long now,' she thought and found she had said it aloud. She shook out her hanky and pressed it gently to her daughter's sweating temples, first one, then the other. If there was any feeling left in the poor child's body, she thought she might enjoy the cool sensation of the well-ironed cotton on her fevered skin.

'Go on,' she added, as Shuna took another spasmodic breath. She might have been encouraging her to jump into a swimming pool or let go at the top of a playground slide. 'Go on. I'm here.'

And she found she was counting past thirty, past fifty. She allowed herself a little cry. Shuna's eyes were already closed – Shirley had not seen them open in the four days since the phone call – but she reached out and gently closed Shuna's mouth. The lips were cracked and looked sore. She took the jar of Vaseline from the bedside cupboard and rubbed a little on them with her forefinger. Then she opened the window and walked back along the corridor to the visitors' room, the crepe soles of her light summer shoes squeaking on the vinyl floor.

Karl, the nice boy from the charity, with the earring, had finally persuaded Arthur to stop pacing, sit down and drink a cup of tea. He sprang up as Shirley came in. Arthur merely raised frightened eyes.

'It's over,' she told them. 'She's gone.'

'Christ,' said Arthur.

Karl came over and gave Shirley a hug, which was nice. She had

131

not been hugged in years. He was a polite, clean boy and probably good to his mother.

'Arthur, do you want to go in for a bit? Say goodbye?' she asked. Arthur merely shook his head, swallowing the tears that had begun to mist his eyes.

'Need a fag,' he muttered and pushed out of the swing door and onto the balcony.

'Do you mind if I do?' Karl asked.

'Be my guest,' Shirley told him. 'She'd have liked that.'

'Have you told the staff yet?'

'No,' she told him. 'Would . . . Would you mind, Karl?'

'Course not,' he said.

As he padded sadly out, she admired again his leather boots with the funny little chains and rings round the heels. She sighed, made herself a cup of tea at the hospitality table and joined Arthur on the balcony. He too, she could tell, had had a little cry. She was glad. Men could be so bottled up.

Shirley stood beside him in companionable silence for a while, admiring the view of Chelsea stretching away from them. She could see the pumping station in the distance and, beyond that, just before the view melted into summer haze, Westminster Cathedral.

'She picked a beautiful day to go,' she said. It was a thin, silly thing to say, she knew, but it was true and she felt it needed saying. The remark slipped into the silence between them which absorbed it like dark water about a stone. When Arthur finally turned to her, it was with a face like thunder.

'Why'd she have to get such a dirty disease? As if what she was wasn't bad enough.'

'Now Arthur, you remember what Karl told us: it's not dirty, it's just a –'

'What's a pansy like that know?'

'I think he knows rather a lot, actually. I think he's already lost several of his friends.

But Arthur was not listening.

'Why'd she have to do it to us?'

'She didn't *do* anything to *us*, Arthur. She caught a virus and she died. If anything happened to us, we did it ourselves, as well you know.'

He rounded on her, his face suddenly tight with fury.

'Shut your fucking hole,' he hissed.

Shirley turned away, angry in turn. He knew how she disliked unnecessary language. He was not really angry. He was upset. Perhaps he had not had a little cry after all. Not a proper one. He would tell it all to Bonnie when they got home; he had always told his Jack Russell the things he could not tell her, mostly things to do with the mysterious workings of his heart and a few other besides. She would send the two of them out to the allotment, say she needed the house to herself while she organised funeral cakes and sandwiches and so on. Death always made people want to stuff their faces. And drink. Juno at the Conservative Club could probably find her way to slipping her a case of that nice sherry cut-price.

'When do you think we can go?' Arthur asked her, in a softer tone – the nearest he would come to an apology.

'There'll be forms to sign, probably,' she told him. 'That's all. And she'll have some things for us to take away or throw out or whatever.'

'Well let's get it over with then we can catch the three-thirty before the rush hour starts.'

'No, Arthur.'

'What?'

'We've got to sort out her flat.'

'Are you mad?'

'It's Shuna's flat.'

'She only rented it. Anyway, it sounds like more of a bedsit.'

'Yes, but she lived there for eight years and I've never seen it and there'll be things to be sorted out there.'

'Leave it, Shirley. Leave it all. She didn't have anything valuable.

You can be sure of that. And what there is the landlord can have in case she was behind with the rent.'

'Shuna was always meticulous about debts. That nice friend of hers said so that visited yesterday.'

'That mangy tart, you mean.'

'Arthur!'

He snorted, holding open the door for her into the visitors' room. Ordinarily Shirley would have sighed and acquiesced, but not today. Her mind was made up.

'Well you can do as you please,' she said. 'She's our daughter and I'm going to do right by her. Honour her.'

'Honour!'

'You catch the three-thirty. I'll come home when I'm ready. I might even have to spend the night.'

'You'll do no such thing.'

'I'll do what I have to do. There's food in the fridge. You know how to work the microwave. You'll survive. You're a cold bastard, Arthur, and one day it'll catch up with you.'

'Shirley!'

'You can sign all the forms for me and bring back her overnight bag and whatever. You've done nothing else of use these last few days.' Shirley was utterly calm in her rightful fury. Karl was waiting for them at the nurses' station. 'Shall we be off, Karl! I need some fresh air.'

'Of course, Mrs Gilbert.'

She turned as they waited for the lift and took a short, hard look at her husband. She would never leave him. They fitted together now like two old shoes and divorce was grotesque in a couple over fifty. There were times, however, when she blithely contemplated murder.

She had taken the keys earlier. They were lying in the bedside locker beside an unopened carton of long life fruit juice and a bottle of Chanel No. 5, which may have suited Shuna, but which Shirley had never greatly cared for. Keys were important, personal things, unlocking secrets, disclosing treasures. She had picked these ones up instinctively to distract her while Shuna was having a long needle pushed into her arm and had forgotten to replace them. They had an interesting fob – a big, silver hoop, like an outsize curtain ring – which felt pleasingly heavy and cool in the hand. Now, as they travelled down in the lift, Shirley's fingers clasped on the bunch of metal as on a talisman.

'Shall I give you both a lift to the station?' Karl asked when they reached the lobby.

'Mr Gilbert's going to the station,' she told him. 'I'm not. I want to see her flat. Would you take me?'

'Of course. But I haven't got keys.'

'I've got keys,' she said and he gave her a quiet but twinkly little smile and she knew at once how his young life was probably rooted in small, harmless deceits and acts of sly kindness. 'Thanks,' she added. 'You're a good boy, Karl. Are you going steady with someone?'

'Yes,' he said and blushed a bit. 'Three years, now, but he's in the army, so I haven't seen much of him lately. He's out in Bosnia.'

'Ah,' she said, adding, 'that's nice,' foolishly, because she was uncertain what to say.

Karl's car was a Mini, black as sin with zebra-striped fur covers on the seat.

'It's okay,' he assured her when he saw her hesitate at the open door. 'They're ironic.'

They had received a phone call from Karl. That was the first they knew of it.

'Hello,' he said. 'You don't know me and officially I shouldn't be contacting you, not without her permission, but she's too sick to talk now and I know she'd want to see you. And I think you've a right to see her too before it's over. She doesn't have long, you see.'

They could not stay at an hotel because neither of them liked being away from home and now, more than ever, they needed the comfort of a nightly return to the familiar, so they came in on the train every day at some expense. They had spent the night this last night, however, marking out the long vigil with cups of watery tea from a vending machine and mournful bars of chocolate. Karl had done all the talking. Arthur was struck dumb, first with grief at the sudden *fait accompli* of her terrible condition, her wasted skin hanging on her protruding bones, her death's head eyes, and then with his understanding of what she had become.

Karl was diplomacy itself. He spoke strictly in terms of the disease and how it was only a disease and not a moral judgement. He illustrated from the depressing scrapbook of his recent memories the deadly impartiality of its appetite. He encouraged Shirley to talk too, asking her about Shuna's youth.

'There's so much she never told me,' he said. 'So much I'd love to know.' He was skilful, well-trained at drawing people out. He was a volunteer assigned months before to befriend Shuna. Shirley thought it strange and rather sad that her daughter had so few friends that new ones had to be trained and assigned to her.

The revelation for Arthur, confirmation of what Shirley had known all along, came on the second day at the hospital, when a woman called in on the ward to see Shuna. She was unnaturally tall, with an astonishingly unlifelike red wig and thigh-length leopardette high-heeled boots. And she wore a perfume which lingered, cutting through the hospital smells long after her brief, tearful appearance, and spoke to father and mother alike of moist, unspeakable things. After she left, Arthur, staggered, finally found his tongue.

'Who in Christ's name was *that*?' he asked Karl as she slunk away up the ward, for all the world like some pagan goddess bestowing dubious blessings. Karl had seemed utterly unfazed, kissing the woman tenderly on the cheek and leading her to the bedside with a kind of courtesy.

'Oh, that was Ange. Angela. She and Shuna work together. Used to, I mean.'

'But she's a . . . ! You mean *my* daughter was . . . ?' Arthur had a rich vocabulary of insulting terms, especially for women, but for once in his life he seemed unable to name names. Karl helped him out.

'Yes, Mr Gilbert. Shuna was a sex worker.'

And Arthur must have believed him because he was too crushed to pick a fight.

It was funny how names changed the way one looked at things. *Sex Worker* had an utter rightness in Shirley's mind. It was truthful, unadorned; a woman's description. Sex was work, hard work where Arthur was concerned, a strenuous matter of puffing and panting and getting hot and flushed and sticky and trying hard to concentrate and not let one's mind make that fatal drift onto wallpaper choice and obstinate claret stains. She had been not a little relieved when he granted her an early retirement about the same time he had his degrading little fling with Mary Dewhurst at the golf club. Shirley was sure that Arthur was more appalled at his late discovery of how his daughter had paid for her generous Christmas presents and fancy imitation fur coat than at her cruel and senseless early death. Sure of it. But she did not greatly care. As her mother used to say: it did not signify.

It took them a long while to drive the short distance across the park and even longer to find a parking space. London had been taken over by cars; smelly, useless things.

'It gets worse every week,' Karl told her as he failed a second time to snatch a parking space and Shirley imagined car upon car clogging the already scarcely mobile queues until a day was reached when no more cars could get in or out of the place. It would become known as the Great Standstill or Smoggy Tuesday. People would die from the poor air quality, children preferably, and finally something would be done, something sensible like persuading men it would not hurt their sexual prowess to ride a bus occasionally.

Shuna's flat was in an unexpectedly leafy square with big plane trees, a well-kept residents' garden and glossy front doors. As she clambered up out of Karl's Mini she realised she had expected something sordid; wailing children in rags, women drunk at noon, surly menfolk with too many rings. This amused her and she laughed softly.

'What?' Karl asked.

'Nothing,' she said. 'Just being silly. Is this hers?' She pointed down to a basement with a tub of flowers outside the door.

'Yes.'

'I should know the address,' she said, 'but she didn't like me to write. I rang sometimes, when Mr Gilbert was out, but I always seemed to get other people – that Angela probably – and I don't think they passed on my messages. Here.' She pulled out the keys. 'You do it.'

Karl took the key ring, looked at the fob, and smiled sadly. 'I bought her this,' he said. 'In San Francisco.'

'Where the bridge is?'

'That's right. It's not really a key ring.'

'Oh? It makes a very good one. Is it for napkins or something?'

'No. No, it's a . . . a . . .' Karl seemed uncharacteristically bashful.

'Is it something rude, Karl?' Shirley helped him out.

'Yes,' he said, grinning. 'Very.'

'Well that's nice,' she told him. 'She must have liked that.'

'She did.'

As Karl turned to unlock the door, Shirley looked at the swinging hoop again, unable to stop herself wondering what on earth such a thing could be used for that would not be extremely painful. He opened the door and she followed him in.

'Good carpet,' she noticed aloud. Shuna had liked carpets as a child, had spent hours rolling around on them as she read or watched television.

'The rent's paid until the end of the month. We've been paying it for her while she was too sick to work. So it's not a problem.'

'You and your guardsman friend?'

'No, no.' He smiled. 'The charity.'

She nodded, beginning to take in her surroundings, the calm colours, the lack of pictures or ornaments, the single, big potted palm behind the sofa. Arthur had been right – it was little more than a bedsit – but it was a very comfortable, well decorated one. Shirley now felt the presence of her grown-up daughter intensely and was shy in the stranger's presence.

'It's very tidy,' she told Karl in a stage whisper, as if Shuna was just around the corner. 'She never used to be tidy.'

'Oh, er, I've been cleaning for her.'

'That's kind of you.'

'Not really, I like to clean.'

'You're very good at it. Shall I make us both a cup of tea?'

'Yes. No. You sit down. I'll do it. Oh God.'

He had paused, his hand on the kettle lid, and quite suddenly was overcome, hunched over the fridge. Shirley touched his shoulder gently. He turned and she drew him to her.

'I'm sorry,' he stammered. 'It suddenly hit me.'

'Don't,' she said. 'It's all right.'

He cried heavily for about ten minutes. It came over him in waves, little surges of grief that she could feel in the tightening of his arms about her. He smelled of leather, soap and man; she liked that. Apart from his brief hug in the hospital, she had not held anyone in years. She did not think she had ever held someone in a leather jacket. She let her fingers stray over its rich, studded surface and stroked the back of his head, where his hair was cut so short she had glimpsed a little strawberry mark underneath it. When he felt better and pulled gently away from her to blow his nose, she felt as relieved as if she had wept too.

'Sorry about that,' he said. 'I should go.'

'Must you?'

'I ought to pop into work, just to check on the mail and things . . . Can I pick you up later?'

'It's okay,' she said. 'I'll probably find my own way to the station when I'm ready.'

'My number's by the phone there, in case,' he said. 'You can

139

take it with you and ring me from home, if you've a mind to.' He kissed her softly on the cheek and left. Nice boy.

She made herself a cup of tea. She explored the flat. She lay on Shuna's bed, even slipped between the sheets for a few minutes. She ate some chocolate biscuits from a tin and played a tape of strange music that was in the machine by the bath. Then, feeling she should do what bereaved relatives do, she reluctantly opened the big fitted cupboard, found a suitcase, and began folding clothes in it to take to the local charity shop. Shuna had developed a good eye for clothes, that much was swiftly evident, a good eye and expensive taste. They were of a size, and Shirley tried on a jacket and coat or two, wondering whether she would ever dare wear something with a famous Italian label and run the risk of Arthur's guessing where it had come from. Then she took out a hanger with the strangest garment on it she had ever seen.

It was black, and so glistening that Shirley thought at first it was a black plastic dustbin liner draped to protect something precious. Then she realised that the black plastic was the thing itself; the dress, garment, whatever. It was quite thick, almost like leather, and shiny as a taxicab in the rain. It appeared to be a kind of all-in-one or catsuit, not unlike the things she had seen ice-skating men wear on championships televised from Norway. It had long sleeves and long legs. It was shaped with reinforcements to form a pointy bosom and, strangest of all, had built-in pointy boots and long-fingered gloves. Shirley could not resist putting one of her hands into a sleeve and into the empty finger pieces. It was extraordinary. The plastic clung to her, seeming to become an extra skin. There was not a breath of air inside. It fitted her arm exactly and shone so, even in the dim light from the window onto the area steps, that it was a surprise not to feel wet. She turned to look in the mirror, fascinated as she flexed and turned her fingers and forearm this way and that. Then, as she pulled her arm out, the garment gave off a sudden scent that might have been Shuna's very essence. With a little gasp, Shirley dropped it on the bed as though it had stung her. She stared at it for a moment, then tried to resume her packing, but its gleaming blackness burned a hole in the corner of her vision. It *would* not be ignored. At last, it proved too inviting and she found herself stripping entirely naked. One could see at a glance that this was *not* a garment for sensible underwear.

MARTIN AMIS

The Information

How can one writer hurt another where it really counts – his literary reputation? This is the problem facing novelist Richard Tull, contemplating the success of his friend and rival Gwyn Barry. Revenger's tragedy, comedy of errors, contemporary satire, *The Information* skewers high life and low in Martin Amis's brilliant return to the territory of *Money* and *London Fields*.

'Any other writer would kill to reach this high style. Amis can stroll the heights at his leisure – the writing is on fire.'

ALLISON PEARSON, *Independent on Sunday*

Martin Amis's novels include *The Rachel Papers*, *Money*, *London Fields* and *Time's Arrow*. His non-fiction includes *Einstein's Monster* and *The Moronic Inferno*. He lives in London.

JUNE   £6.99   PAPERBACK

The Information

IT WAS MIDNIGHT. Richard sloped out of his study and went to the kitchen in search of something to drink. Anything alcoholic would do. He experienced a thud of surprise, from temple to temple, when instead of the usual striplit void he confronted his wife. Gina was not a large woman, but the mass of her presence was dramatically augmented by the lateness of the hour. And by marriage, and by other things. He looked at her with his infidel's eyes. Her oxblood hair was up and back; her face was moist with half-assimilated night-cream; her towel dressing-gown revealed a triangle of bath-rouged throat. With abrupt panic Richard realized what had happened to her, what she had done: Gina had become a grownup. And Richard hadn't. Following the pattern of his generation (or its bohemian wing), Richard was going to go on looking the same until he died. Looking worse and worse, of course, but looking the same. Was it the kids, was it the job, was it the lover she must surely have by now (in her shoes, in her marriage – if Richard was married to Richard, *he'd* have one)? He couldn't object on grounds of ethics or equity. Because writing is infidelity. Because all writing is infidelity. She still looked good, she still looked sexual, she even still looked (you had to hand it to her) . . . dirty. But Gina had made a definite move towards the other side.

'I was thinking we might have a progress report,' she said. 'It's been a year.'

'What has?'

'To the day.' She looked at her watch. 'To the hour.'

145

Relief and recognition came together: 'Oh yeah.' He had thought this might have something to do with their *marriage*. 'I got you,' he said.

He remembered. A close and polluted summer night, crying out for thunder, just like this one. A late emergence from his study in search of drink, just like this one. A dressing-gowned and surprise-value manifestation from Gina, just like this one. There were probably one or two differences. The kitchen might have felt a little brighter. There might have been more toys about. Gina might have looked a day or two younger, back then, and definitely ungrownup. And Richard might have looked a bit less like shit than he looked now.

That time, a year ago, he had had a very bad week: the debut of Gwyn Barry in the bestseller list; the striking of Marco; Anstice; and something else.

This time he had had a very bad year.

'I remember.'

He remembered. A year ago to the hour, and Gina saying,

'How many hours a day do you spend on your novels?'

'What? Spend?' said Richard, who had his whole head in the drinks cupboard. 'I don't know. Varies.'

'You usually do it first thing, don't you. Except Sundays. How many hours, on average. Two? Three?'

Richard realized what this reminded him of, distantly: being interviewed. There she sat across the table with her pencil and her notebook and her green tea. Pretty soon she would be asking him if he relied, for his material, on actual experience or on the crucible of the imagination, how he selected his subjects and themes, and whether or not he used a word-processor. Well, maybe; but first she asked:

'How much money have they earned you? Your novels. In your life.'

He sat down. Richard wanted to take this sitting down. The calculation didn't occupy him for very long. There were only three figures to be added together. He told her what they amounted to.

'Give us a minute,' she said.

Richard watched. Her pencil slid and softly scraped, then seemed to hover in thought, then softly scraped again.

'And you've been at it for how long?' she murmured to herself: good at sums. 'Right. Your novels earn you about 60 pee an hour. A cleaning lady would expect to make seven or eight times that. From your novels you get a fiver a day. Or thirty quid a week. Or 1,500 a year. That means every time you buy a gram of coke – which is what?'

He didn't know she knew about the coke. 'Hardly ever.'

'How much is coke? Seventy? Every time you buy a gram of coke . . . that's more than a hundred man hours. About six weeks' work.'

While Gina gave him, in monotonous declarative sentences, a précis of their financial situation, like something offered to test his powers of mental arithmetic, Richard stared at the tabletop and thought of the first time he had seen her: behind a tabletop, counting money, in a literary setting.

'Now,' she said. 'When was the last time you received actual payment for your novels?'

'Eight years ago. So I give them up, right?'

'Well it does look like the one to go.'

There followed a minute's silence – perhaps to mark the passing of Richard's fiction. Richard spent it exploring his own numbness, whose density impressed him. There were surf sounds in his ear. Emotion recollected in tranquillity, said Wordsworth, describing or defining the creative act. To Richard, as he wrote, it felt more like emotion invented in tranquillity. But here was emotion. In his room across the hall Marco was pleading in his sleep. They could hear him – pleading with his nightmares.

She said, 'You could review more books.'

'I can't review more books.' There on the table lay a slablike biography of Fanny Burney. Richard had to write 2,000 words about it for a famously low-paying literary monthly, by next Friday. 'I already review about a book a day. I can't review more. There aren't enough books. I do them all.'

'What about all this *non*-fiction you keep agreeing to write? What about that Siberia trip?'

'I'm not going.'

'I don't like to say this, because at least it's regular, but you could give up *The Little Magazine*.'

'It's only a day a week.'

'But then you spend for ever writing those "middles". For nothing.'

'It's part of the job. The literary editor has always written the middles.' And he thought of their names, in a wedge, like an honours board: Eric Henley, R. C. Squires, B. F. Mayhew, Roland Davenport. They all wrote the middles. Richard Tull. Surely you remember R. C. Squires's controversial attack on the Movement poets? R. C. Squires was still alive, unbelievably. Richard kept seeing him, in Red Lion Street, in the callbox, staring with illegible purpose at the crowded entrance of the language school. Or flapping around on his hands and knees in the passage behind the Merry Old Soul.

'For nothing,' said Gina.

'Yeah that's right.'

'No one reads *The Little Magazine*.'

'Yeah that's right.'

One of Richard's recent 'middles' was about writers' wives – a typology of writers' wives. The pin was a biography of Hemingway, who, Richard argued, had married one of each. (Stoutly or fogeyishly resistant to clever headlines, Richard had in this case submitted to the inevitable 'For Whom the Bells Toll'.) How did they go? The Muse, the Rival, the Soulmate, the Drudge, the Judge . . . Of course there were many, many others. Peer Wives like Mary Shelley, and Victim Wives like Emily Tennyson, and Virgin Saints like Jane Carlyle, and a great multitude of Fat Nurses like Fanny Stevenson . . . What type was Demeter Barry? What type was Gina Tull? Transcendence-Supplier, Great Distracter, Mind-Emptier in the act of love. Anyway it didn't matter. Gina was deciding to absent herself from the company. She wasn't leaving Richard, not yet. But she was ceasing to be a writer's wife.

'You can't give up the Tantalus thing, which is pretty decent as well as regular. You tell me. You could give up smoking and drinking and drugs. And clothes. It's not that you spend. You don't earn.'

'I can't give up novels.'

'Why not?'

Because . . . because then he would be left with experience, with untranslated and unmediated experience. Because then he would be left with life.

'Because then I'd just have this.' The kitchen – the blue plastic tub filled with the boys' white pants and vests, the stiff black handbag on the chair with its upturned mouth open wanting to be fed, the bowls and spoons and mats laid out on the table for the morning and the eight-pack of cereal boxes in its cellophane: all this became the figure for what he meant. 'Days. Life,' he added.

And this was a disastrous word to say to a woman – to women, who bear life, who bring it into the world, screaming, and will never let it come second to anything.

Her eyes, her breasts, her throat, showing him his mistake, all became infused. 'The possible alternative', said Gina, 'is I go full time. Except Fridays of course.' She told him what they would pay her: a chastening sum. 'That'd mean you getting the twins up every morning and get them down every night. The weekends we share. You shop. You clean. And you cook.'

'I can't cook.'

'I can't either . . . That way,' she said, 'you'll be getting plenty of life. And we'll see what you've got left for the other thing.'

There was a third alternative, Richard reckoned. He could fuck her twice a night for ever and take no more shit. And have no money. Oh sure: do it that way. He looked at her face, its flesh lightly glazed in preparation for sleep; and her throat, with its weathered complexities of raisin and rose. She was his sexual obsession. And he had married her.

'I tell you what,' she said. 'How close are you to finishing the one that's on the go now?'

Richard creased his face. One of the many troubles with his novels was that they didn't really get finished. They just stopped. *Untitled* was already very long. 'Hard to tell. Say a year.'

Her head went back. This was steep. But she took in breath and said, 'Okay. You've got a year's grace. Finish that and we'll see if it makes any money. I think we can hold on. Financially I mean. I'll do what I have to do. I'll manage. You've got a year.'

He nodded. He supposed it was just. He wanted to thank her. His mouth was dry.

'A year. I won't say a word.'

'A year,' Gina now resumed. 'And I haven't said a word. Have I. I've been as good as my word. What about you?'

Nasty repetition that, he thought: word. But it remained true enough. She had kept her promise. And he had forgotten all about it. Or he'd tried. They had held on, financially, though even the most perfunctory calculation told Richard that they were falling short by two or three book reviews a week. Marco was still in his boxroom, and still remonstrating with his nightmares.

'What's your progress been? Is it finished?'

'Virtually,' he said. This wasn't quite true. *Untitled* wasn't finished exactly, but it was certainly unbelievably long. 'A week or two away.'

'And what are your plans for it?'

'I was thinking,' said Richard. 'There are these minor earnings from my novels that we didn't include. It all adds up, you know.'

'What all adds up?'

'Things like PLR.' He checked: Gina was staring at him with a new order of incredulity. 'Public Lending Right,' he went on. 'Money from libraries. It all adds up.'

'I know PLR. With all the forms. How much did you get that time? The time you spent the whole weekend lying down behind the couch. What was it? Thirty-three pee?'

'Eighty-*nine* pee,' said Richard sternly.

'. . . Well that's a big help!'

There was a silence during which he steadily lowered his gaze to the floor. He thought of the time when his PLR cheque had burst into the three figures: £104.07. That was when he had two novels in print and it was still the case that nobody was sure they were shit.

'I think I've got an agent. Gwyn's agent. Gal Aplanalp.'

Gina took this in. 'Her,' she said. 'Have you signed up?'

'Not yet. Maybe soon.'

'Hey this is really going to *happen* you know. You don't care about money and that's a nice quality but I *do* and life is going to change.'

'I know. I know.'

'. . . What's it called anyway. Your new one.'

'*Untitled.*'

'When will it be?'

'No it's *called Untitled.*'

'You mean you can't even think what to call it?'

'No. It's *called Untitled.*'

'How can it be *called Untitled?*'

'It just is. Because I say so.'

'Well that's a bloody stupid name for it. You know, you might be a lot happier, without them. It might help with the other thing too. It might be a big relief. Gwyn and everything, that's a whole other story.' Gina sighed, with distaste. She had never liked Gwyn much even in the old days, when he was with Gilda – and they were *all* poor. 'Demi says it's *frightening* the way the money comes in. And she's rich! I don't know if you still really believe in it. Your novels. Because you never . . . Because what you . . . Ah I'm sorry, Richard. I'm so sorry.'

Because you never found an audience – you never found the

universal or anything like it. Because what you come up with in there, in your study, is of no general interest. End of story. Yes: this is the end of your story.

'Marry your sexual obsession,' Richard had once been told. By a writer. Years ago. Marry your sexual obsession: the one you kept going back to, the one you never quite got to the end of: marry *her*. Richard was interviewing this writer, so it more or less followed that he was neither famous nor popular. His obscurity, in fact, was the only celebrated thing about him (let's call him Mr X): if everything went through okay, he had a chance of becoming a monument of neglect, like a Powys. How many Powyses *were* there? Two? Three? Nine? Your sexual obsession, he kept saying: marry *her*. Not the beauty, not the brains. Mr X dwelt in a two-up-two-down back-to-back, in Portsmouth. The stuff he wrote was hieratic and recondite, but all he could talk about was sex. And sexual obsession. There they sat, at lunchtime, in the dockside pub, over their untouched seafood platters, with Mr X sweating into his mac. Don't marry the droll brain surgeon. Don't marry the dreaming stunner who works in famine relief. Marry the town pump. Marry the one who does it for a drag on your cigarette. Richard felt his shoulders locking. By this point he had readied himself to face a full nervous breakdown of sexual hatred – a complete unravelling, an instantaneous putrefaction of bitterness and disgust. But it never quite happened. Marry the one who made you hardest. Marry *her*. She'll bore you blind, but so will the brain surgeon, so will the dreaming stunner, in time . . . Dropping the writer off after lunch in the minicab, Richard hoped for a glimpse of his wife. Hoped for a chance to wonder what *she* was: rocket scientist? hysterical goer? The woman staring suspiciously down the damp dark passage, her small head half lost in the sprouty collar of her housecoat, didn't look like an hysterical goer. She looked more like a rocket scientist; and one whose best work was long behind her. And another thing: whatever life choice Mr X had gone ahead and made, Mrs X didn't strike you as too happy about it either, contemplating her husband's return, it seemed to Richard, with infinite weariness. He was forgotten now anyway, or reforgotten, silent, out of print. He never even made it into Neglect ... Some of us, most of us, all of us, are staggering through our span with half a headful of tips and pointers we've listened to (or overheard). Use Cold Water To Soak The Pot After Making Scrambled Eggs. When Filling A Hot-Water Bottle, Keep The Neck Of The Hot-Water Bottle At Right-Angles. Unless The Kettle Boiling Be, Filling The Teapot Spoils The Tea. Starve a cold, feed a fever. Banks do most of their business after three o'clock. Richard married his sexual obsession. He just did what he did.

Except in one important respect, the love life enjoyed by Richard and Gina, over the past year, remained as rich and full as it had ever been. There was still that sense of anticipation when nightdress and pyjama conjoined, last thing, and, at weekends, when they stirred, and at other stolen moments, such as they were, with two little boys in the house. Gina was a healthy young woman. Richard was in the prime of life. After nine years together, their amorous dealings were, if anything, even more inflexibly committed to variety and innovation than at any point in their past. The only real difference, I suppose you'd have to concede, was that Richard, nowadays, was impotent. Chronically and acutely impotent. Apart from that, though, things were just as they were before.

He was impotent with her every other night and, at weekends, in the mornings too – when those boys of his gave him half a chance! (The patter of tiny feet; the stubborn and inexpert worrying of the doorknob; the hoarse command from the bedroom met by puzzled whispers, puzzled withdrawal; the mindfilling silence before the sickening impact or collision – the scream, the wail.) Sometimes, when the Tulls' schedules conspired, he would be lazily impotent with her in the afternoons. Nor did the bedroom mark the boundary of their erotic play. In the last month alone, he had been impotent with her on the stairs, on the sofa in the sitting-room and on the kitchen table. Once, after a party outside

Oxford, he had been impotent with her right there on the back seat of the Maestro. Two nights later they got drunk, or rather Gina got drunk, because Richard was already drunk, and on their return from Pizza Express stole into the communal garden, using their key, and Richard was impotent with her in a sylvan setting. Impotent, in a sylvan setting, under some dumb blonde of a willow, with Diana above them, her face half-averted, feeling wounded or betrayed, and higher, much higher, the winking starlets of the Milky Way.

It got so bad that Richard talked – and even thought – about giving up drinking: he even talked – but didn't think – about giving up smoking. He knew, though, that his troubles were dully and intricately and altogether essentially literary, and that nothing would ease them except readers or revenge. So he didn't do anything, apart from taking up Valium and cocaine.

'It's hard on you. It's like an ultimatum,' said Gina in the dark.

Richard said nothing.

'You're tired. And you've got a lot on your mind.'

Richard said nothing.

WENDY PERRIAM

Coupling

Beattie's lover Max has given her a very special birthday present – a weekend at England's most exclusive health farm. But if he had known what was to happen there, he would have bought her a diamond instead. For thirty-year-old Beattie, who has always fancied men, suddenly finds herself attracted to a woman – a woman twenty years older, cultured, privileged, a mother of four, a grandmother, even. Beattie's initial infatuation erupts into a passion which threatens to take over her life as, desperately, she seeks admission into Elizabeth's inner sanctum – her work as a psychotherapist, her family, her very soul.

Wendy Perriam's genius at putting ordinary people into extraordinary situations is seen to brilliant effect in this intriguing story of obsession, sexual confusion and, ultimately, redemption, as Beattie moves beyond jealousy to forgiveness and self-fulfilment.

Wendy Perriam was expelled from a strict convent boarding-school and escaped to St Anne's College, Oxford, where she read History. After a stint in advertising and a succession of more offbeat jobs, ranging from the bizarre to the banal, she now writes full time.

JULY   £15.99   HARDBACK

Coupling

'RIGHT, THIS IS IT!' the tractor-driver shouted as he swung left off the road, then phut-phutted laboriously through the elaborate wrought-iron gates. A heraldic crest soared overhead and proud stone lions reared on either side. 'I'll take you up to the house, shall I? It's still a fair old haul, by the looks of it.'

'No, I think I'd better . . .' Beattie's words were shredded by the wind. She abandoned all attempts to speak and clung grimly to the side of the trailer as it bumped and rattled up the drive. Her other hand clutched her makeshift hood – an old fertilizer bag the man had offered her as protection against the elements. The rain was drumming down as relentlessly as ever, drenching her best clothes; her once-blue skirt now darkening into black.

A sudden hooting made her jump. A chauffeur-driven Mercedes, immaculately white, had nosed up behind them and was trying to overtake. She ducked down out of sight – too late. The passengers had spotted her and were bound to gossip about the dishevelled girl they'd seen, delivered at the Grange by trailer like a bale of sodden straw.

Once the car had passed, she raised her head and peered out at the formal landscaped gardens sweeping down to an ornamental lake, complete with statuary and fountain. Ashley Grange was *grand* – which made it all the more ridiculous to turn up draped in plastic sacking with a weatherbeaten yokel as her chauffeur. She kept wanting to laugh – or cry.

The tractor negotiated the final bend and spluttered to a halt outside the house. It was every bit as imposing as the grounds: row upon row of windows, a green-domed roof, and an entrance

157

flanked by fluted marble columns. A second set of supercilious stone lions stood rampant at the bottom of the steps and another pair guarded the front door – lean and sinewy beasts, looking as ravenous as she was, as if about to devour the heraldic shields they held. Perhaps they'd come as a job lot, she thought – a whole pride of lions going cheap. Nothing else was cheap, least of all the cars, parked in snooty rows outside the house: Rolls-Royces and Range Rovers, a vintage Jaguar and several long, low, restless sports cars chafing at the bit.

The man clambered down to help her out of the trailer. 'How the other half live, eh?' he muttered, with an attempt at a smile.

She leaned on him and jumped, landing with a thud, feeling the hardness of the gravel through her flimsy white suede shoes. She was dressed for this morning's sunshine, not the Noah's Flood which had erupted after lunch.

The man heaved her suitcase down for her, shaking the rain from what little hair he had. 'Want a hand with this inside?'

'No, honestly, I'm fine now.' She wasn't a snob – far from it – but she was already very late, and the last thing she wanted was to walk into this mansion accompanied by a tattooed and balding chaperone in streaming oilskins and mud-caked rubber boots. She was being observed as it was. A scarlet Lotus had pulled up alongside and its two female occupants (impeccably turned out – and *dry*) were staring at the tractor in astonishment. Beattie hunched over her bag, unearthed her purse and pushed a five-pound note into the tractor-driver's hand. 'Thanks – you saved my life!'

Before he could respond, she was running towards the entrance and up the marble steps. As she reached the top, she heard the tractor revving up to leave, and for a moment she was tempted to dash after it.

No *way*, she told herself. Don't be so pathetic. Get in there and go for it!

Decisively she walked inside; cold greyness giving place to bright lights and near-tropical heat.

She found herself in an elegant reception hall with floor-length velvet curtains and a marble fireplace surmounted by a flamboyant antique mirror. A bevy of gilt cherubs beckoned from its frame. She took a step towards them, caught sight of her reflection and quickly looked away. Her suit was clinging wetly to her body, and her expensive hair-do had been reduced to dripping rats' tails. Selfconsciously she wiped her feet, aware of a group of women lounging on a sofa, talking with that loud assertive confidence born of wealth and breeding. And mounted on the wall behind them was a display of large signed photographs: celebrities who had stayed at Ashley Grange. Perhaps you *had* to be rich and famous to be admitted here at all.

She edged towards the reception desk. 'Beattie Bancroft,' she mumbled, aware that the name sounded bogus – which it was. 'I . . . I'm sorry I'm so late. My car broke down, miles from anywhere, and I couldn't find a phone-box. Is there a garage I can contact?'

'Don't worry, madam. We'll take care of that. If you could just tell me where you left the car and let me have the keys . . .'

Beattie suppressed a grin. She couldn't quite imagine her battered, fourth-hand 2CV, with its dented bumpers and rusting bodywork, sitting intrepid amidst the pedigree cars outside. Still, she had no wish to leave the poor thing stranded in some lonely country lane all night. She handed over the keys, then filled in the registration form.

'Thank you, Miss Bancroft. You're in the Bluebell Room – just off the Grand Staircase. The porter will show you up. I'm afraid you've missed your consultation, but we can slot that in tomorrow.'

'Consultation?'

'With Matron.'

Beattie pushed a strand of wet hair out of her eyes. Had she come to the wrong place – a boarding school or hospital?

'We like our guests to have a brief medical check-up on arrival, to monitor their blood pressure and so on, before we schedule any treatments. And talking of treatments, I see you were booked to have a massage at five, with Julie, but I'm afraid you've missed that too. All the staff will have left by now.'

'Oh bloody hell! I could really use . . .' Beattie broke off in embarrassment. Bad language seemed a crime in these surroundings. Two haughty-looking women were standing just behind her and must have overheard. Max might have done better to have given her a subscription to the RAC, rather than a weekend at an exclusive health farm.

'I'll see what I can do for you, Miss Bancroft.' The receptionist glanced up from her appointments book with a lacquered smile which failed to reach her eyes. 'If you'd like to go to your room and change, I'll phone the treatment suite to see if anyone's still there. You might just be lucky, you never know.'

'Thanks, that's great. I really would appreciate it.'

She followed the porter – and her damp-stained case – along a stretch of corridor and up a curving staircase. Everyone she passed seemed to be female and in pairs. She wished *she* had come with someone, but none of her friends could have afforded the inflated prices, and Max himself would never fit in here. Max was to blame for her language: *he* swore all the time and she had picked up the habit almost without noticing. She didn't actually disapprove of swearing (it was only words, after all – a combination of syllables which meant nothing very much), but it annoyed her that he should influence her so strongly. He had also paid for her new slinky suit, which she now realized was out of place. The Ashley Grange dress-code was studiously casual: designer tracksuits; no make-up beyond a natural healthy glow.

The porter stopped to unlock a panelled door and ushered her inside. She wondered if she should tip him, and how much. Health farms were probably a law unto themselves. She slipped a pound coin into his hand, quickly scrabbling for a second coin when his inscrutable expression failed to thaw into a smile.

Once he'd gone, she stood gazing at the room: bluebells everywhere – and *frills*. The frilled bluebell-patterned bedspread

matched the ruffled bluebell curtains, and there were more bluebells on the wallpaper and more frills on the lampshades (which
were mercifully plain blue). The room was so large it was a fair
trek to the window, which looked out over miles of mist-swathed
countryside – majestic, even in the rain. What an ungrateful bitch
she was, turning her nose up at the bluebells, when this was the
most luxurious place she'd ever *been* in – a world away from her
London flat, where nothing matched at all and which overlooked
a row of dreary garages. Perhaps she should ring down to reception
and order an improvement in the weather. It was only the first
week of September, and only ten to six, but instead of golden
lushness it was as murky as a wet November night.

She rubbed the misty windowpane and watched the wind slap
the shivering poplars, freckled with their first brown leaves. She
had seen Christmas cards already in a shop in Westbourne Grove.
Ninety-six shopping days to Christmas. No, she mustn't think of
Christmas – it posed too many problems, such as how to put the
'happy' in it, where to spend it, and who with.

She walked briskly back to the bed and unlocked her case. This
was meant to be a *break*, for heaven's sake, and anyway it was
pointless worrying about Christmas four months in advance. Far
better to unpack and change her clothes.

Her stomach rumbled suddenly as she kicked off her wet shoes.
She should have brought emergency supplies: a litre of Bacardi, a
crate of Crunchie bars. She hunted through her handbag, but
found only a lone toffee, which she unwrapped guiltily. Sweets
were bound to be forbidden at a health farm – as were alcohol
and smoking, according to the brochure. What if there were
hidden video cameras, spying on her right now? Well, one
Creamline toffee was hardly an indictable offence.

She drifted into the bathroom, wincing at the array of mirrors.
No cherubs here to recoil from her; just that unflattering reflection
staring back again. Her hair still looked unspeakable and she'd
clearly overdone the henna. It might be an idea to have a shower
– wash off some of that vulgar red; wash off the last two hours.

She was just unzipping her wet skirt when the phone rang. Max! He said he'd ring at six. She ran to pick up the receiver, her skirt sliding to her ankles. 'Darling,' she said, speaking indistinctly through the toffee. 'This place is quite amazing! I've even got . . . Oh, sorry. I thought . . .' She dislodged the toffee from her teeth, hastily spitting it into her hand. 'Gosh, thanks. Where do I go? And – oh – what am I supposed to wear?'

A robe? She hoped her towelling dressing-gown fitted the description. Slippers she'd forgotten, so it would have to be bare feet.

Ask for Steve? A *man*? She hadn't thought in terms of male masseurs. In fact, she had never had a massage in her life, but had assumed it would be given by one of that glamorous breed of females who staffed most beauty parlours – all hair and bones and eyelashes. The idea of Steve was somehow disconcerting, as if he were appraising her already, judging her too fat, too naff.

'I thought you said you'd booked me with . . . er, Judy?'

'*Julie*. Yes, but I'm afraid she left at half past five. Don't worry, Steve's absolutely first rate – one of our best masseurs. You'll be in very good hands, I assure you.'

'Okay,' she said nervously, reaching for her 'robe' and sucking the last sinful trace of toffee off her teeth. 'I'll be right down.'

* * *

'*Relax!*' urged Steve. 'You're incredibly tense.'

'Sorry,' Beattie murmured, her face pressed into the couch. Though why should she apologize for a stiff back and knotted shoulders? Anyway it was impossible to relax when she kept worrying that her body might smell sweaty. She should have had that shower.

'Just let go. That's better. If you tense your muscles, it's more difficult for me to work.'

She shifted on the couch. Odd to think of it as work. Steve

162

might be working – battling with her recalcitrant muscles – but *she* just had to lie there beneath thick white fluffy towels. The room was frilled again and blue again (though delphiniums this time, not bluebells) and partitioned into cubicles, each lit with blue-shaded lamps. All the other cubicles were empty; the only sound Steve's soothing voice and some schmaltzy music playing in the background.

'How long are you here for, Miss Bancroft?' He accompanied the question with a slow sweeping movement down her spine.

'Just the weekend.'

'And have you been to Ashley Grange before?'

'No. Never.' It sounded rather abrupt. He was only trying to be friendly, after all. 'Actually, it was a birthday present,' she added, her voice muffled by the couch. She needn't say *which* birthday. She dreaded being thirty – the official end of youth, that terrifying watershed dividing the successes from the failures. If you hadn't made it by thirty, you probably never would. She wondered how old Steve was. It was difficult to tell. His formal manner and starched white uniform were at odds with his boyish figure and exuberant fair hair.

'Aha!' he laughed. 'A present from your boyfriend, I bet.'

How on earth had he guessed? Why not from her mother? Except her mother was dead, and would have given her bath salts, or a box of 'useful' notepaper, not a weekend of indulgence.

'Sort of,' she hedged. Max was far too old to be called anybody's boyfriend. He said he was forty-nine, but she suspected he'd been forty-nine for a couple of years at least. He seemed touchy about his age, so she didn't like to question him too closely, especially as she'd only known him three months.

'Is that painful?' Steve was asking, as he pressed a knobbly bone in her spine.

'Ouch! Yes.'

'I'm not surprised. You've tensed again. Do try to relax.'

'Look,' she said irritably, 'it's not *easy* to relax. I've had a hell of a day. I got hopelessly lost on the way here and landed up in the back of beyond. Then my car broke down and . . .' Suddenly she was pouring out the whole demoralizing saga.

'God! It sounds horrendous.' His hands had moved to the back of her neck, and were slicking deftly out across her shoulders. 'Never mind – now you're here, you can take it easy. This is the perfect place to unwind.'

Obediently she let her body sink into the couch; tried to stop herself from thinking altogether and just enjoy the first massage of her life. She closed her eyes and surrendered to the sensations: the fragrant smell of massage oil, the soft blue glow of light, Steve's firm, confident touch. She wished he wouldn't talk so much – it was an effort to keep having to reply – but masseurs were presumably trained, like hairdressers, to avoid silence at all costs.

'Have you come far, Miss Bancroft?'

'No, only from London. Just off Westbourne Grove. I've always lived in London – well, except for my first sixteen years, which I spent in dreary old Croydon. Mind you, I suppose even that's considered part of London now.'

'Croydon? Really? That's where my parents live.'

'Gosh, I'm sorry – I hope I didn't sound rude. Which part?'

'Highfield Road.'

'Oh, yes, I know it. *We* weren't quite so grand.' She could see the house quite clearly in her mind: a poky terraced house which seemed always to be dark and cold, even in the summer. And somehow always empty – her father away, her mother ill upstairs. As a child, she had invented her companions; transforming the bad-tempered kitchen boiler into a rumbustious grandfather, spitting words and flames, and then cancelling him with a candy-floss-haired grandma who made her currant buns. Weird how she could remember tiny details – her mother's china chamber pot with its yellow crusted scum inside; the purple knitted tea-cosy coddling the brown teapot; the way the bathroom door squealed, as if it were constantly in pain.

'Right, Miss Bancroft, if you'd like to turn over . . .'

She opened her eyes, annoyed with herself for wasting time in

Croydon, breathing in boiler fumes instead of scented oils. Steve held the towels discreetly over her while she rolled over onto her back. All along he'd been meticulous about covering the parts of her body he wasn't actually working on. None the less, it was rather an unsettling experience to be lying completely naked, alone with a strange man in a remote wing of an unfamiliar house. The massage must be halfway through, yet still she hadn't managed to let go. She took in a deep breath, exhaling with a long yawning sigh.

'Tired?' Steve asked sympathetically.

'Yeah, I must admit I am. I've been working late all week. *And* last weekend. And I got up at the crack of dawn this morning, so I could leave the office early.' Dammit – she was here to forget the pressures. There were two delicious days ahead without a deadline in sight. She wrapped the thought around her like a luxurious goose-down duvet and at last felt her body relax. It was more comfortable in any case lying on her back. Her face was no longer squashed against the couch, and the crick in her neck had gone. She hardly even cared now about not having had a shower, but simply lay contentedly, savouring the sense of peace, the cosseting. Steve was massaging her foot, gently kneading the ankle, devoting time and trouble to each toe. Bones she didn't know she had were being discovered and defined; her whole body stirred by his expert touch. *Max* never touched her like this – he was too concerned with his own pleasure – but Steve was a professional. He was also damned attractive, in a different league from Max; his body lean and muscly, and conspicuously defined by his closely-fitting jacket and white trousers.

'And what work is it you do, Miss Bancroft?'

'Look, do call me Beattie. It makes me feel so ... *ancient* when people use my surname.' She blushed, wondering if she had sounded over-familiar, but it was hard to keep up the formalities now she was beginning to see him not just as a masseur but as a *man*. She noticed the fair hairs glinting on the backs of his hands, and tiny drops of perspiration beading his top lip, which she found peculiarly exciting. Once, she caught his eye, and looked away, embarrassed. His eyes were slatey-blue, with a serious expression, as if he regarded his work as some solemn sort of ritual.

He completed the right foot and folded back the towel to start on her leg – firm kneading movements up and down the calf. His hands moved higher still, gliding up the inside of her thigh. She felt her nipples stiffen; her legs ease surreptitiously apart. God! She mustn't react, or it would show on her face. Massage had nothing to do with sex (well, in Soho strip-joints, maybe, but not in a genteel place like this). Besides, it was disloyal to Max, who was paying for this treatment; paying for the entire weekend. Determinedly she switched her mind to mundane things – stalled engines, rainswept roads – but Steve's hands were only inches from her groin and the tension was electrifying. She let out an involuntary sound: a sort of muffled gasp of pleasure, which she tried to conceal with a laugh. 'I . . . I'm feeling better already, Steve.'

'I'm glad to hear it, Beattie. But do relax. I can feel your muscles tightening again.'

How *could* she relax? She was caught in an impasse, simmering between indulgence and frustration, tension and release; her mind saying one thing, her body another. And anyway she wasn't used to lying back, just accepting and enjoying. Her normal role – with Max, at least – was to give pleasure, not to take it. Yet those ingenious fingers on the inside of her thigh were weakening her resistance. And so was the whole atmosphere: the soporific heat and lulling music, the warm caress of the towels. She wished her face was covered. Surely Steve could see the effect he was having? Her eyes had closed and her neck curved languorously back, as if she were abandoning all control.

She willed him never to stop, to inch his sensuous fingertips higher and higher up her thigh, until they slipped beneath the towel. In her mind it was happening – her legs edging further apart, her whole body arching up, as she whispered 'Yes, go *on*, Steve.'

Then suddenly she realized that he was no longer working on her legs at all. He had moved from the foot of the couch and was now standing by her head. She opened her eyes, to find him looking at her. She didn't glance away this time; instead held his gaze for what seemed dangerously long. It was he who broke the contact, as he transferred his hands to her shoulders and began smoothing out the stiffness there.

'You're very knotted up, Beattie. I hope this isn't hurting.'

'Yes, it is a bit.' She smiled at him – a suggestive smile. 'I prefer the . . . gentler stuff.'

He gave one last sweeping movement along her shoulders, then placed his hands on her collarbone, just above her breasts, pressing firmly against the skin. It felt almost more tantalizing than if he'd touched the breasts themselves. Yet his expression was still solemn and intent, and the towel still irreproachably in place (though she longed to push it off, to seize his hands and force them against her nipples). The same steady pressure continued – provocative, exquisite. Was this a standard part of the massage, or was he arousing her deliberately?

'Steve,' she whispered. 'You're making me feel . . . wonderful.'

He appeared not to have heard. She could see the tip of his tongue just showing between his teeth – he was obviously absorbed in what he was doing; totally preoccupied. More seconds passed, until she was exploding with the tension, then finally, unbearably, he removed his hands and stood upright, with a quick glance at his watch.

'I'm afraid we have to finish now, but your back and shoulders need a lot more work. I haven't managed to break down all those bad adhesions.' He traced a line with his finger from one shoulder to the other, to indicate the problem. 'But I could fit you in later on this evening, for' – he paused – 'a more intensive treatment.'

TRISTAN HAWKINS

The Anarchist

Sheridan Entwhistle, a middle-aged magazine executive develops anarchistic tendencies when a suspected heart attack forces him to reappraise his life. Much to the distress of his bemused wife and outraged neighbours, he goes on an uncharacteristic and very anti-social bender – resigns from his highly paid job, spends a night in the woods in the pouring rain, picks a fight in a pub, wears one of his wife's floral blouses to a barbecue party, and finally teams up with a couple of New Age Travellers on their way to the Glastonbury Festival. The ensuing psychedelic chaos is a brilliantly executed and hilarious look at modern values and suburban attitudes.

'Hawkins can be slick and funny; a writer to watch.'
Independent on Sunday

Tristan Hawkins lives in north London and works in the advertising and publishing industries. He has written one previous novel, *Pepper*, which was published to great acclaim.

JULY   £9.99   HARDBACK

The Anarchist

THERE WAS AN ANNOUNCEMENT.

It began, 'This is an announcement,' then nothing. Then everything crunched to a halt.

The bald man with the lavish ears peered up from his paper and took in the other passengers.

It was bad news.

Insouciant skirts and brave suits. Youth, handsome looks and wealth.

All of them mocking his bad suit and pie crust shoes. Smirking at his simmering blood-bag of a face. And was it possible? – all of them in full knowledge of the *unfortunate episode*.

Perhaps, there could be no question about the bald man with the lavish ears who sat perspiring on the Victoria Line tube train that afternoon.

No question that he was the genuine article. A bona fide sex offender. Your actual nonce. A moral bankrupt cowering in unpressed pinstripe and a noose-fast tie. For why else would his face burn cerise at a stranger's glance?

A pair of recently holidayed legs lay draped in the walkway. Parted arrogantly and wiped across the thighs with little more than the rumour of a skirt, it seemed she was almost daring him to take a peek. Filch a glance at the unpossessable, then at once experience all the wretchedness of his age; his sex; his off the peg, all-weather suit; his Tory broadsheet; his bald head and lavish ears; his everything.

He re-reddened at the inadvertent volume of these peculiar thoughts.

171

Then he swallowed – but the obstreperous, mucoid gas of his throat stayed put. And it seemed to him that he was now wafting outside his body, as if in some other dimension, and that the stubborn gas had transformed itself into a great liquid and the bald man with the lavish ears was now drowning.

In a single spasm he scrunched up his paper and moaned.

A resonant belch of a moan. The clamour of a randy bull-frog. Or a sluggard mastiff. The exhalation of a new corpse.

'You alright, mate?' Someone from this dimension said.

'Yes thanks,' he thought he managed to grunt.

But Sheridan Entwhistle was not alright at all. His entire body was squeezing out sweat and he trembled like a rodent lifted from its cage. His field of vision was fast colliding into itself and his chest felt as if it were being compressed into the mass of ball bearing. And though he was breathing hard, gasping even, the air refused to enter his body. As if deflated, his head dropped and his vision was momentarily sucked along the delicious vale of her thighs.

Then . . . nothing.

When he came to a second or so later he was somewhat giddy yet in full possession of his faculties and his life. Forsaking decorum, he fiddled the pebblish knot of his tie loose and popped open the button below.

The tube wheezed into motion and coughed on to Victoria. Adeptly Sheridan folded up his paper, slotted it into his briefcase and joined the swarm of summer suits and shirts being sucked away by overground trains. And he thought, with mild and deliberate amusement, that apart from a heart attack it had been a rather unremarkable day.

Sheridan flopped down and the cool armchair drank him into it.

'Three, three, five?' A momentary smile zipped under her big nose as she unscrewed the bottle cap.

'Perhaps, I'll refrain tonight,' he said reflectively. Then, not wanting to arouse premature suspicion in his wife, he laughed, 'Go on, just a wee-un then.'

'I,' Jennifer announced as if heralding something she were supremely proud of, 'spent most of this afternoon lounging in our new conservatory.'

'Good God, woman. I'm surprised you're not sautéed.'

'Oh no, darling,' she seemed to echo as if in another room, 'There was the divinest of breezes with both doors open.'

'So now I take it, we're playing host to every airborne bug in Edingley. Charming.'

He slipped a hand inside his jacket and counted the steady, rhythmic beats of his life. Still he couldn't be sure of this. Not with things in slo-mo as they were.

His wife smiled and he smiled back and thought: yes, I'm doing well here.

Tinkling out the pleasant refrain of the outer life with one hand.

Mutely thumping out the discordant base of the inner riot with the other.

He swallowed and forced himself to speak in what he considered was a sufficiently melodious manner.

'Seen much of the Unspeakably Behaved today?' he asked, tunefully he imagined.

'What do you think?'

'Well, it is half term. For some. At Imogen's is she?'

Jennifer handed him the drink, looked hard at him and dragged a vicious hand back through her grey roots. He knew the gesture and raised an eyebrow. Still she said nothing, glaring at him all the while as if she were employing the sight of his face to seethe her anger up to the point of expression. She refocused on the carpet and spoke in rapid stabs.

'Imogen, you say. You mean Imogen, whose mother I happened to bump into in the butcher's today. Who, when I made a polite enquiry about our daughter, took great relish in informing me that they'd just, that very morning as it happened, received a divine postcard from Boston. Not Lincolnshire of course, she simpered over a pound of best mince, the other Boston, you know, the one just west of Ireland.'

'Jennifer, my dear, I hate to say I told you so. But I did say at the time, do try and work on a boy. A lot less heartache. A lot less bloody . . .'

'Well, I'm glad you can take it in your stride.'

'Go on then. Theories?'

'Chromasomically deficient, three.'

'Boy? Man? Men? E.R.E.?'

'Beg pardon?'

'Edingley Rugby Eleven?'

'Yes, of course, Sherry. Flippancy, that's the ticket. I . . . I . . .' Jennifer rose, sniffed shamelessly and marched through the open doors of conservatory. She paused to count something on her fingers, turned and said acidly, 'Indian hemp, nine.'

Sheridan thought for a moment, then moaned, 'C'mon, Jennifer. Now that *is* ridiculous.'

He felt his chest constrict.

She strode back in the living room and clutched the wings of his chair. Defiant of the odd gasp and sob, she declared that, sure as she stood here, she had smelled marijuana on Folucia's clothes *and* in her room *and* in the bathroom. And there was no mistaking it. It *was* marijuana. Besides, was she or was she not, as each day passed, taking on the appearance of – she didn't know: 'One of those New Age whatever-they're-called-s?'

Sheridan waited for his heartbeat to rev down then calmly asked whether Jennifer had any further evidence. She told him that she wasn't sure but perhaps she had noticed a sort of far away look in Folucia's face of late. He reached back, rested both his hands on hers and smiled. He spoke slowly and possibly condescendingly.

'I'll wager my golf clubs against your aspidistra that the Unspeakably Behaved's countenance comes courtesy of a chromasomically challenged, unspeakable whatsitsname; that the whatsitsname is in the singular, and that, in your olfactory ignorance, you are failing to appreciate the subtlest of all-the-rage perfumes, again courtesy of the whatsitsname. Opium or something. That's a perfume, I believe. But, further evidence pending, I shall have a word with the suspect.'

'Sherry, she *lied* to us.'

'She's fifteen, just done twelve rounds with puberty, she's allowed the odd prevarication.'

'Well in my day the age of dissent was eighteen.'

'And well worth the wait I dare say. But times change.'

'Humph. Well I hope you're right, Sherry. Well, sort of. But you know how I loathe disturbances. Anyway, how was work today?'

'Oh, expletive dash faecal matter, four.'

Coronary thrombosis, more commonly known as a heart attack is the result of a blood clot (thrombus) which impedes blood flow in one of the coronary arteries . . . Symptoms range from intense discomfort in the centre of the chest . . . shortness of breath . . . giddiness . . . cold sweat . . . occasionally loss of consciousness . . .

He raised a hand, laid it softly on his ribcage and swallowed the panic like a hard boiled egg.

The book remained half open, suspended temporarily at an uncomfortable right-angle. He found it mildly disconcerting – a taunting metaphor for his mortal limbo. He shook his leg and the volume shut with a damp thud.

Sheridan closed his eyes and inhaled several times, attempting to bridle the demented fission of his thoughts. Naturally the notion of the G.P. substantiating his suspicions was a horrifying one. But, he considered, once past the forty mark the hoodwinking was quite certainly over. Any man believing he's still in some way young after the watershed is either a coward or a fool. So the G.P. it had to be. And by God, Sheridan Entwhistle would enter and leave that surgery with a smile. Even if a dry throated, *thank you, sir, for flogging me,* smirk was the limit of it.

He stood cautiously and timidly walked over to the bookcase. Again he raised a hand to his chest.

'Eleven o'clock and everything's well,' he murmured to himself and slid the family health manual back into its gap. Sheridan smiled to himself. There could be no doubt that he was a brave man and it pleased him. But as he turned to leave and join his wife upstairs he was struck by a notion that pleased him even more.

Like hell, would he visit the G.P.! He'd imagine that it had never happened – and innocently notch up his life assurance. Then he'd think about seeing the bloody doctor. Now, *that*, Sheridan considered, was brave.

The *unfortunate episode* surfaced once more. He tucked it beneath the covers of his consciousness and went up to bed.

ANN OAKLEY

A Proper Holiday

A proper holiday should offer sun, sea, and escape from the trials and tribulations of the day-to-day. As their mother winds down by the pool and their father is distracted by Meg in her dreamy golden bikini, teenagers Jade and Star sense their chance for excitement and adventure.

Breezy and engaging, this deft comedy of manners takes a refreshingly unsentimental look at family life, the exuberance of youth and the complexities and hypocrisies of middle age.

Ann Oakley is Professor of Sociology at the University of London. She is the author of four novels, including the international bestseller, *The Men's Room*.

JULY   £15.99   HARDBACK
£5.99   PAPERBACK

A Proper Holiday

THE COALS OF the barbecue heated up and the smell of charred flesh mixed with that of the bougainvillaea and the women's perfumes. 'It makes me feel sick,' confided Star to Aaron. 'It's quite unnecessary to eat animal flesh, don't you think?'

'Not to mention the environmental pollution,' observed Aaron, sniffing.

'If we go to the beach we mustn't disturb the baby turtles.' Star was torn by conflicting motives: excitement and adventure, on the one hand, and environmental concern, on the other.

'Fuck the turtles,' retorted Joshua. 'The earth's a cruel place. And it belongs to us.'

'You mean us particularly?'

'I mean us particularly.'

Star looked up. The half moon that was there seemed incredibly bright. But then the air was clearer here than in south Hampstead; the moon's light had less to contend with trying to make its imprint on the earth.

'Are you coming, Aaron?' Star sensed a kindness and a stability in him that was missing in Joshua Holbeach. Her own temperament and her role as Jade's shadow led her to be cautious.

'Might as well.' Aaron, too, was bored by the proceedings tonight. He'd rather have been at home in W6 with his mates, or reading books about the new techniques of chronometric dating, including amino-acid racemization and thermoluminescence. If his mother hadn't been so obviously otherwise engaged, he'd have suggested a moonlit trip to the ruins the other side of the river, which they'd not yet visited. But he could see from here that all her attention was being taken by that Star and Jade's father. On the whole, Aaron took a philosophical view of his mother's relations with men. When he'd been younger, he'd felt threatened, but now he'd learnt that the men come and go. One of them might be the flavour of the month for a while, but they never last. Meg said she wasn't very good at living with them and there was always a point at which living together came up. Aaron could see what she meant. His mother had some pretty unsavoury habits, like taking all her paperwork and many of her meals to bed. She'd got a little portable television by the bed and a two-bar electric fire and a succession of very expensive boxes of chocolate Bath Oliver biscuits. She got up a nice chocolate-y fug. And then there was her housekeeping style – or rather the lack of it. That was why they didn't seem to have any of the normal 'why-don't-you-clear-up-your-room' sorts of rows other parents and teenagers had. Sometimes Meg would say to him despairingly (standing in the living room or the kitchen), 'We've got to do something about this place, Aaron!' And then the two of them would put their gas masks on and get the black plastic sacks out and grapple with the ancient Hoover (a leaving present from one of the men) and reward themselves with a take-away crispy duck and pancakes.

Aaron's friends envied him his laissez-faire mother. Sometimes he envied them their live-in fathers. But whenever he got close, he saw the down side: the rows, the competition, the marriages about to break up, or just held together because-of-the-children. At least I'm no excuse for anything, he told himself. And then there were the social work stories his mother brought back: abandoned home-alone children, seriously hit women, blokes who squandered the dole on beer and never had anything that hadn't come off the back of a lorry, women who did the streets to feed their kids – it made your heart bleed for the human race, except that race was racist and his mother's social work department was good on equal opportunities, as it was cheaper to clean up your language than anything else.

'Come on, let's get some food organized.'

Star and Aaron, Joshua and Jade, Kelly and Simon piled their plates and took a heap of paper napkins, and Jade went round to Kizi and whispered something in his ear about doggie bags. At first Kizi didn't understand (not many Americans came here) but then he went off to the kitchen and came back with some heavy-duty paper bags.

Portia Holbeach, in attendance on her sick mother, saw all this provisioning going on from the window of her mother's room. 'I'm hungry, Mum,' she said. 'Can I go and get something to eat?'

'Of course, darling, I'll be all right for a bit.' Grizelda felt as though an army had been sitting on her stomach. She was full of kaolin, which made her feel even heavier, and had just taken some codeine for her headache, which would succeed in bunging her up even further.

'What are you doing?' hissed Portia to Jade.

'Be quiet! We're going on a little expedition.'

'Can I come?'

Jade looked at her witheringly.

'We did promise,' Star reminded her, thinking of the glasses.

'Oh well, I guess so.'

'We can't all leave at once,' said Joshua, 'they'll get suspicious. I'll go first. The rest of you should leave at five minute intervals. We'll meet down by the harbour. I'll go and hassle for a boat.'

Thirty minutes later a boat that could have been a fishing vessel, but wasn't, silently passed the bright lights and animal smells of the Hotel Rhapsody Palas. Sitting at a table close to the river's edge, Crispin and Meg saw the boat, but thought nothing of it. The other side of the pool, sitting sideways on two sunbeds gnawing their way through thick lamb kebabs, Ronald and Sandy licked meat juices off their fingers without a thought for their own parental responsibilities. Derrick Upton was entertaining Lisa and the honeymooners to an imitation of John Major; Lisa had seen it before, but she enjoyed other people thinking Derrick funny. Also, Derrick had told her before they left their room that evening that he'd been doing some sums and they'd be able to afford both his nose job and her sky blue runaround after all. Nothing made Lisa happier than the prospect of spending money.

Joshua had persuaded the Karput boat co-operative to let him pilot the boat himself. The money that he'd taken from his father's wallet helped. Josh had learnt boating at his school. Joshua Holbeach was good at lots of things, but particularly those involving some manual or physical skill. What he'd really like to be is a master craftsman making fine objects out of wood.

'D'you think he knows what he's doing?' whispered Star to Jade.

'Of course he does, silly.' She admired the masterful way Joshua was standing there moving the – what was it called? The tiller. She couldn't imagine her father behaving like that – taking control, working out what to do and then doing it.

At first Joshua stuck fairly closely to the river bank where there were lights, so he could see what he was doing. Then, when they went round the corner and Karput and the hotel disappeared from view, he switched on the battery-operated lights on the mast of the boat.

'This is great, isn't it!' said Simon Upton, a little nervously.

'When can we eat?' Portia was still starving, and when she was hungry that was all she could think about.

'When we get there.' Fortunately it wasn't difficult to get to the sea. There were no wrong turns to be made; only the tracks of the dark reed-spattered water to be followed. It was cool out here in the river; the night air was mixed with a fierce salty breeze. Joshua dragged his pullover from the bottom of the boat.

'What was that?' Kelly was startled, her eyes rounded, by a harsh sound from the reeds.

'Probably a marsh frog or a terrapin. Nature's a noisy thing.'

Jade went to stand next to Joshua at the helm. He put his arm round her. The boat swerved. 'Watch what you're doing!' rebuked Kelly sharply. 'Cut the lovey-dovey stuff, for God's sake!'

When they reached the mooring platform by turtle beach,

Simon jumped out with the rope. They tied up the boat and took their bags of food. The beach was dark and empty of everything except for the outlines of chairs and tables and folded umbrellas, which picked up what moon- and starlight there was. Far away, it seemed, the sea rippled with patches of etiolated light, advanced and receded with a gentle lunar pulse. Joshua turned on a torch. 'Put that off,' instructed Star sharply.

'Aw, come on.'

'I mean it. There's enough moonlight to see by.'

'For us, or for the fucking turtles?'

'Both.'

Joshua dropped the torch in the boat. It wasn't worth fighting over.

'It's cold.' Portia shivered.

'Here, have my jacket.' Aaron handed it over, and added, to cheer her up, 'You never know, we might turn up your glasses!'

They took the food down nearly to the water's edge and sat down in the damp sand. Jade handed it out. It was hard to see in the semi-light. Star got a piece of meat by mistake and flung it in the ocean in disgust.

'Hey, that's good nutrition! There are people in the third world who'd be glad of that.'

'This is the third world,' she pointed out.

'Okay, okay. We don't want no political lectures now.' Joshua bent forward so the juice from his kebab dripped on to the sand. Kelly opened a can of Pepsi. 'We can do better than that.' He took two half bottles of vodka out of his pocket.

'Where d'you get those?'

'Dosh. Dosh reaches things nothing else does.'

Jade unscrews the first bottle and tips it to her lips. The bottle catches the light, which is reflected back on the whiteness of her face and neck against her black hair; the black sky, the cavernous ebony ocean. Joshua rips the bottle from her, laughing. 'Two can play at that game!' He falls on top of her; they tumble and twist in the sand. The others turn away. Aaron looks apprehensively at the sky, where clouds are blotting out the light of the stars. They'd left a light on the boat running, so they could find it again. He wonders how long the batteries will last.

Joshua stands up. 'Who's for a swim, then?'

'We haven't brought our bathers.'

'Who cares?' He strips down to his Calvin Klein underpants. Everyone looks away except Jade. 'Come on, Jade, come in with me.' He slips an arm round her waist, begins to wrestle with her t-shirt.

'I don't think you should, Jade,' protests Star. 'You've only just eaten. You know Mum says we shouldn't swim straight after eating.'

'Mummy's girls are we?' mocks Joshua. Jade lifts the vodka bottle to her lips again. Joshua pulls her shorts down. She stands there on the beach in bra and pants. Joshua begins to kiss her. She throws her white neck back.

'Stop it!' shrieks Portia suddenly. 'We don't want a sex show!'

Joshua turns to her and laughs. He takes Jade's hand and together they walk into the sea.

'You don't want to swim, do you?' Aaron asks Star.

She shakes her head, looking, he thinks, rather desolate. 'I think I'll go in with them, just to keep an eye on things.'

She nods. 'Thanks, Aaron.'

It is by now quite clear that something is happening in the sky: the clouds are slowly but surely organizing themselves into a storm. It's been threatening for days, with weather which even for southern Turkey has been oppressively hot. The revellers back at the Hotel Rhapsody Palas's Proper Holidays barbecue notice it. Kizi points: 'The Gods will be angry tonight.'

'"Angels mumbling", my mother called it.' Meg Shaw takes two glasses of wine back to the table by the river. She gives one to Crispin. He holds it up, as though inspecting it for imperfections.

'I love you,' he says, hardly looking at her.

'Nonsense,' she replies, in her best social worker voice.

'I do, I do,' he moans. 'I can't get you out of my head. Ever since the first day of the holiday, when I saw you diving into the pool in your golden –'

'– yellow M and S,' she interrupts.

'Shut up, bikini. I've been obsessed by you since then.'

She sits back in her chair, laughing. 'Crispin, you're a married man here on holiday with your wife and two daughters. Your life is with them.'

'You don't understand,' he pleads, reaching for her hand in the thundery darkness. 'I've not felt like this since I was a teenager. I feel alive. Life is full of hopes and meaning. I want you, Meg! I want to be a part of you. I want to be joined to you. I want to join my life to yours. I want to make love to you in the moonlight, in the starlight, in the sunlight, in the everything light.'

Above them, the first rumble of thunder is heard.

'Looks like the evening's coming to a premature end,' remarks Ronald Dunkerley to Sandy Holbeach. They have migrated to a more comfortable seat to the right of the barbecue, overlooking the pathway into Karput, and the place where the local river-crossing boats are moored.

'I'd better go and check on the children,' says Sandy.

Ronald nods. He admires responsible motherhood in a woman. 'Can I get you anything while you're gone? More coffee? Wine? A cognac, perhaps?'

'That would be nice.' She smiles at him, and a strand of her glossy hair escapes its confines on top of her head and falls over her shoulders, covering her seashell ear, but revealing her vulnerability anew. It occurs to Ronald that he'd like to see all of her with all her hair down.

Kizi and the other staff are beginning to clear up the barbecue. Bilge and Suleyman are taking the umbrellas down and removing the mattresses from the sunbeds to protect them from the rain. The music pouring from the loudspeakers changes to Gershwin's 'Rhapsody in Blue'. 'Dum der dum,' sings Ronald, drumming on the table with his fingers. He gets up to order the cognacs. The other side of the bar, Crispin Delancey is holding Meg Shaw's hands between his own in a gesture that looks very much like pleading. Ronald feels momentary guilt about Crispin's wife and his own confined to their beds by the gastro-intestinal side-effects of carpet-buying. He slips over to the other side of the pool and opens the door to the Dunkerley room very quietly. Grizelda is asleep. Portia isn't there, but Ronald is sure he's seen her somewhere about recently, eating. So that's all right, then.

Another rumble of thunder, and another. But it's a long way away still. Maybe it's something electric in the atmosphere, but Professor Ronald Dunkerley can't bear to think of the evening ending just yet. Why, it's only just begun. Here he is, sitting with an attractive young(ish) woman, for the first time in God knows how long, on his own, in a highly romantic setting, and what is he going to do about it?

'Would you like to go for a midnight swim?' Ronald asks Sandy, as they sip their cognacs.

She almost chokes on hers. 'Where? What, in this weather?'

'We could take that boat' – he points to the nearest of the hotel rowing boats – 'and go across the river, and swim from there. The river's quite clean.'

'Are you sure?'

'Oh yes.' He smiles kindly at her in a manner not unlike the one he uses for explaining to the college accountant that not everything in academic life can be measured in terms of money.

Back on turtle beach, the youth club is also responding to the electric current in the air. Jade and Joshua are behaving like badly tutored porpoises in the waves, and Aaron is admonishing them with threats of being struck by lightning. Portia and Star have cleared up the food. Simon is digging in the sand evilly looking for turtles' eggs, and Kelly is working out how she can get her own back on Jade Delancey for stealing Joshua Holbeach from her.

A not-so-distant rumble of thunder is followed by the first flash of lightning, zigzagging in mercurial brilliance across the surface of the navy blue sea. Jade is startled. 'What was that?' Her black hair is joined seamlessly to the waves.

'That was a warning from on high,' says Aaron. 'Telling you it's time to get out. Please. There's going to be a real storm, and we've got to get these kids back to the hotel. If you two aren't coming, we'll go without you.'

'You won't be able to manage the boat.'

'You do learn some things at state schools, Josh.' Aaron didn't say this unkindly, but it's enough to get Joshua out of the sea.

There's another flash of lightning while Jade and Joshua and Aaron turn their backs and struggle out of their wet underclothes and back into shorts and t-shirts. The lightning makes the white flesh of their backs gleam like swordfish. Everyone else is waiting on the boat. Portia is shivering and even Kelly seems a little frightened. Josh looks at all of them. 'Don't be scared, kids, it'll be all right. Uncle Josh'll get you home. In only a few minutes you'll all be back with your mummies and daddies!'

They cast off, and Joshua starts the motor. It won't catch at first, which causes a good deal of breathholding. Then it does, and they're away. Out in the middle of the dark river with only the reeds and hidden birdlife for company, the lightning comes again, dashing across the sky and into the earth prefaced by thunder that feels as though it's going to split the boat . . .

Portia sits very close to Kelly and Simon, who are abnormally silent. And then the rain starts. It's as though everything's inverted, and the river is falling out of the sky. Although Joshua rolls the sailcloth across the top of them, it's intended to cut out the sun, not this kind of liquid beating, which lashes out at everything. 'It's exciting really,' says Simon, looking up at the embattled sky.

'Do you think they'll miss us?' asks Portia hopefully.

'Na. Shouldn't think so.'

They probably wouldn't have done, had an unfortunate collision not occurred between the *Fidan* and the *Tuna I*, the Hotel Rhapsody Palas's number one rowing boat, which is just coming back from the opposite shore bringing the wet figures of Ronald Dunkerley and Sandy Holbeach, who were caught with their pants down in the river when the storm started. Joshua doesn't see the smaller boat in time to stop, and Ronald, who is rowing, doesn't have enough room to reroute the *Tuna I*, even when he has seen the larger boat advancing. 'Oh my God!' Sandy covers her face in the skirt of her wet apricot dress, and Ronald's mouth drops open when he sees who's aboard the *Fidan*, particularly the pale figure of his good daughter, Portia.

MARIANNE WIGGINS

Eveless Eden

Eveless Eden is the story of the affair between Noah John, London correspondent of a New York newspaper, and Lilith da Vinci, international press photographer. Of how they meet in a rain-soaked bar in West Africa, how they fall in love, and how the paradise they make is lost. Because when one of them lets the evil in, there's no going back.

'A memorable and intelligent love story, a thriller set in the world of rapid political change between 1986 and 1991 . . . *Eveless Eden* is quite a heart squeezer. But it is also full of beefy ethical questioning, personal and political, which is why the use of contemporary history as an allegorical framework works so brilliantly.'

HELEN STEVENSON, *The Times*

Marianne Wiggins was born in Lancaster, Pennsylvania, in 1947. She has lived in Paris, Brussels, Rome and New York, and now lives in London. She is the author of four previous novels, and two collections of short stories.

JULY   £5.99   PAPERBACK

Eveless Eden

WE WENT TO THE CRY-DIE.

. . . but first, we met.

And let me tell you, we did not meet cute (as they say in Hollywood), unlike the way she and Adam met, which—if not cute—was certainly dramatic.

The first time I saw Lilith I was standing at the bar in Chez Josette in Yaoundé, Cameroon, with Dick-the-spokesperson from Our Embassy, taking notes about the gas cloud which had erupted from a lake and killed two-to-five thousand people while they slept a few nights before in several villages to the northwest, near Wum.

This was in August, 1986—and the explosion from the lake was on the night of August 21st, to be exact. On that night an enormous lethal submarine gas mass composed of carbon dioxide and hydrogen sulphide had erupted from the depths of Lake Nyos into the atmosphere and rolled, like an invisible lava, down the surrounding foothills, killing in its wake at least two thousand people and twice that many cattle and domestic animals. It had killed the insects, too—including flies—but it had not killed plants, in fact the plants had flourished in its wake, because flora feast on carbon dioxide.

"You mean it was a sort of killer belch?" I asked Dick-the-spokesperson from Our Embassy, trying to get a technical handle on the chemical process.

"More like a fart," Dick answered.

I put down my pen.

This was my first time in Cameroon, and to tell the truth, I was sorry to be there. But when a lake explodes (farts/belches) and kills thousands of people and your paper wants you to be there, you go.

As it happened, I was in Geneva on another story and I flew from Geneva direct to Yaoundé on Swissair—a bit of the ol' magic djinn at its best, weaving the journalist's luck, because to have flown from anywhere else in Europe that week would have been a hellride into the seacoast capital, Douala where it was raining god's cats and dogs. Yaoundé was dry.

Africa was never my beat.

It was pure chance that I was in Geneva in a week when everyone else who had more experience to cover an African story was taking home leave or was gripped by the shits or was tired or lost or stranded in Chad. So I went.

Maybe I should tell you what it's like to land, solo, in a place you've never been, to get a story. It's hell; but it's a known hell, after you've done it most your life.

The first thing that you need to do is to find someone other than yourself who speaks your language, who can describe this new hell to you in terms that you can almost understand.

You never know who this "someone" will be—but, most likely, this first time, this "someone" will be the first camel driver you meet who speaks your language, or the "Information" official at the airport who inspects your papers, or the Press Officer from the local government or the Press Officer from *your own* government, or an unemployed university student, or a pimp, or a desk clerk, or a concierge, or a money changer or a thief, or a drop-dead-dramatic lady with a heart-breaking come-on, or a cop. If you're lucky, you'll stop with the camel driver.

In Yaoundé I was lucky, because that part of Cameroon had wrested independence from the French, and I spoke a little French. Also, it was the official capital of the formerly un-unified Cameroons, so the relatively savvy Ewondo and Fulani and Bamoun and Bamiléké at the airport sized me up and looked me over and herded me, like collies on an errant ewe, into the One Car That Was Meant For Me, driven (of course) by a man called Ahmadou, namesake-for-democracy-in *tout*-Cameroon.

One long taxi ride to my hotel on Mont-Fébé and sixteen phonecalls later, I was standing at the bar, surrealistically acclimatized, in Chez Josette near the U.S. Embassy in the Place de l'Indépendance, having not yet taken any measure of the city or the country, smelled its alleys, seen its mists and dawns—I was standing at the bar in Chez Josette with Dick-the-spokesperson from Our Embassy, interrogating him about The Event for history, mom, and all the eager readers hanging on my every word Back Home.

"Jog?" (I thought he said.)

"—sorry?" (I think I answered.)

". . . you-*jog*?" he said.

"Ah, no," I answered.

"That's good you won't get shot."

"I won't get—?"

"—shot. Kid last year—nice kid, from California—got up in the morning and went jogging. Normal. Five o'clock, so what? Still dark. Jogged around the Presidential Palace. Boom."

". . . um, could you tell me a bit more about the explosion on the lake—"

"So I wouldn't go jogging around the Presidential Palace if I were you."

". . . I won't."

". . . the police here don't really want to shoot you, they're just looking for some extra money. False arrest for bribes—that's the pattern—false arrest and bribes—it's quite a business. You'd be surprised how many times we're called just because most of our nationals don't know how to spring themselves from jail . . ."

I began to look around the bar, thinking I would like to spring myself from Dick if I could find another source for information. Chez Josette was not a place designed along the classic lines of Rick's American in *Casablanca* with its pale walls and airy spaces —Chez Josette felt *squeezed*, somehow, close and cramped despite the ubiquitous ceiling fans, even though the crowd dribbling in from Embassy Row was still thin. Then it dawned on me the bar had been constructed at the wrong height. The bar was at waist level. Next to it, I must have looked like a giant. Dick looked like a giant too.

"—most of them were sleeping," Dick was saying. "Went to sleep and never woke. Imagine that. Asphyxiated in your sleep. But a lot were still awake—it was a market day. A lot of people wait for night—the coolness—to make the journey home from market. And they say . . . I mean, the reports are, those people just fell down. Dropped in their tracks. Smelled the smell of rotten eggs—that would have been the sulphide—smelled the smell of rotten eggs, felt a warm sensation and passed out. Around nine thirty. Suffocated, just like that. Never knew what hit them.'

". . . a '*warm* sensation'?"

"—warm."

"—what is that?"

"—you don't know what a 'warm' sensation is?" Dick asked.

"—*why* the 'warm' sensation?" I amended.

". . . apparently a symptom of that kind of suffocation. You'll have to ask somebody from the WHO . . ."

"The WHO are here?"

"Crawling with the WHO. Crawling with all kinds of *médecins*. Lots of French. And lots of Catholics."

"Any present danger?"

"No one knows for sure."

"Was WHO the first relief team in?"

"—no, the Swiss were. Missionaries. Crawling with Swiss missionaries. Saw it from their helicopter . . . *Hélimission*."

"Survivors?"

"Not very many. Town was packed, because of market day. People in from Lower Nyos . . . Subum . . . Cha. Those were the villages worst hit. And Fang. Crawling with Save the Children people there, too. Scavenging for orphans. You ought to do a piece on them. That's the piece you ought to do. On NGOs—a piece on all the non-governmental organizations doing business here. CARE. Someone ought to do a piece on CARE's influence on this continent—talk about cultural intervention! That's the piece I'm waiting for someone to do."

I had stopped taking notes the instant Dick had started sounding like Captain Kirk aboard The Enterprise. You get these civil servants talking and the next thing that you know they've told you most of their frustrations and their fantasies. Their frustrations are usually along the line of too little or too much "cultural intervention", and their fantasy is to tell you how to do your job.

"I thought Cameroon was actually one African nation feeding itself, producing enough food—free from CARE, in other words,' I humbly submitted.

"Oh you *have* done your homework," Dick assessed. "I suppose I don't have to tell you, then, how Cameroon got its name . . ."

I signalled the bar man for another (what else?) Coke for Dick and switched, myself, from Primus (brewed by Heineken in Zaïre) to the much lauded Gala brew from Chad. My antennae told me my djinn had let me down, Dick was not going to develop into the perfect source (the perfect source would have asked me to his home tonight, cooked me a great meal, revealed state secrets and introduced me to El Presidente's wife . . .)

"*Camarões*," Dick was saying, "*camarões* means 'shrimp'. When the Portuguese came here they called this country *cameroon* for all the shrimp they found . . ."

Whereas the English would have had the sodden sense to name the country after one of Us, a familiar voice boomed behind me. "And while we're on the subject—can anyone explain this *ripping stench*?"

I turned around, and there was Duff.

He was, as always, at the center of his own mess, but there in Chez Josette he looked particularly disgraceful—tie, well, *burned*, actually, shirt, as usual, two-thirds out of his pants, a jacket that was probably white linen beneath its encrustation, florid face and tousled hair, dusted, this time, by a substance much like cornmeal. And of course, as ever, drunk.

He had with him a similarly drunk white male whom I determined to be Duff's imperfect source from Their Embassy.

"I told you," Duff's imperfect source was detailing, "it's fecal. Flying. Dust."

"That's right," Dick said. "Flying *fecal* dust, actually. Deadly new. It's a sort of space age cholera."

"It gets in your lungs," Duff's person said. "Where—oddly—you can't smell it . . ."

"But when it starts to rain," Dick said, "which it does every evening here this time of year for about an hour—then you can really smell it—it *is* fecal, after all—and it stinks up everyone and everything it falls on—"

"Including crops?" I asked.

"Fuck the crops," Duff roared, "what I want to know is is it going to *kill* me? Because if it's going to kill me I'm not going down alone . . . If it's going to kill me I demand that it kills Noah, too, in the spirit of true non-lateral the fuck agreement . . . Hallo, Noah. Good ol' Noah. Why the fuck are *you* here?"

Because *it's happening, baby*, I said.

"Fucking fart lake, is it?" Duff focused, falling somewhat toward the bar, where he demanded, "What the hell is this, something out of Munchkinland?" and ordered up a double gin. He clapped a swollen pink hand, like a mullet, on my shoulder and looked at me slyly from the corner of his eye. "What you and I should do," he stage-whispered, "is lose these flat-earth people, halve the cost of some local muleteer for the morrow and hie ourselves to Wum for a co-national inspection."

Absolutely, I agreed, that's what we should do, Duff, I said, trying not to have to prop him up.

"Now tell me more about this fecal flying matter," he announced to everyone in general while attempting to ignite a sodden match to light his cigarette. "I ought to warn you, though," he broadcasted, inhaling god-knows-what, and then exhaling eerie ochre stuff, ". . . *I am a journalist*."

Which was true, technically, though by then Duff had become

a shadow of his former self, a caricature of what he had once been. He did not 'report', as such—he wielded language as a weapon. He was deadly clever and the slick sheets paid him large for dishing British royals and Brit expats around the pools in Hollywood. He looked the part of Richard Burton in the movie *The Night of the Iguana*—always sporting that sad linen jacket that wouldn't button over an open-throated beef-fat-cum-*pistou*-stained collegiate shirt missing several buttons two-thirds tucked into a waistband over which a roll of alcoholic-calories-made-flesh pushed a moraine of bodyfat ever downward toward his center of the universe. His diction, rolling like a thunder over plummy wastes of some lost dialect, commanded everyone's attention, but I had known him long enough to know that if you hitched your towline to his dizzy elocutions he would drag you back and forth across a single latitude on stale wind. It was always better to avoid him on assignment in the larger world beyond saloons—but in saloons he was great company, although I had to wonder why he'd come to Cameroon, why he'd landed in, as Bogey says about Rick's place in *Casablanca*, "a saloon like this". No one was gambling much of anything in Chez Josette—not a single *laissez-passer* was for sale, it was the fag end of a (fecal) dusty August day in Africa, about to rain, there was no Claude Rains in sight and I was standing at a midget bar with one drunk Brit and several shitheads from as many embassies on the rue du Cercle Municipal in a former French colonial backwater where the hotels are all called Indépendance, de la Paix, Impérial or Terminus, where, across the street, I could get a sheepmilk-and-goatmeat Croque O'Burger or a korma-and-teriaki at one of the many Indian-&-Nip joints, and I was there to get the angle and the motive and the background into focus to transmit my so-wise and essential tidbits of What's Happening to London and thence to New York to land at your front door tomorrow morning—when, of all the gin joints in all the towns in all the world, she walks into mine.

Duff was having a go at some Frenchman who had caught his bloodshot eye at a nearby table, "Feel free," he was saying, "to speak in French when you can't think of the English thing to say, but answer this before you do, please, because I am a journalist: Is there *any* nation on this earth whose citizens consume as many frogs as yours?" when in she came.

She swept in, really, like a gust of weather, her entrance stage-managed to perfection like (to fuck this metaphor completely) a Puccini heroine, like Mimi or like Butterfly, whose melody is heard off-stage before we see her face. There was a high-pitched commotion at the door of Chez Josette behind a set of weather curtains, then an adjunct (one of Ours), scurried towards Dick and Duff *et moi* and stopped in front of Dick and said, "I'm sorry, sir. The Africans insist. There's been a mix-up, sir. Two of their policemen. And a child."

"'A child'?" Dick said.

"A girl, sir," came the answer, "*one of ours.*"

With that, all heads at the bar at Chez Josette turned toward the entrance as the curtains broke and in swept two of Yaoundé's Finest hustling between them a slim something, soaking wet and cursing, stinking of fecal dust, dressed in nothing but a yellow plastic poncho to the middle of her thighs, and a pair of rubber thongs.

It was the get-up, studiously devised, that made her look, at first glance, like a child—that, and the size of her head, which was small with small features (except her eyes), and the way she wore her hair (short and sleeked back.)

Her eyes were (and are) lighthouse-lamp-size.

Her legs were (and are) *fantastic*.

They seemed to start at her armpits.

They were long, long from hip-to-knee-to-anklebone, and smooth, with not a bubble on them—and as she was hustled in, between *les flics*, she appeared to grow so that by the time she reached Dick and *moi* and Duff and several Frenchmen who had stood up from their table, she no longer seemed a girl. This is Lilith's gift—she is the mistress of a million guises. Or, to put it as a bad cliché—she can assume the form of any woman, any time, for anyone. Or so I thought. But I'm the last person you should trust to tell you about Lilith because I was—from the beginning —utterly in thrall to her.

Timing, as we say in the scoop business, is everything.

Maybe I was ready to fall hard for any woman who showed up at that hour—or maybe, as Isak Dinesen would have it—it was *Africa*. But I fell facedown into the alphabet soup, the c-d/e-f— *coup de foudre*.

Level-headed Southern boys shouldn't handle lightning bolts, they shouldn't play with *coups de foudre*—not before their suppers —because their preachers and their playwrights teach them *coups de foudre* lead straightaway to broken hearts and crimes of passion. Level-headed Southern boys, like stately plump buck mulligans, should stay sober, marry wisely and invest their money in legumes. They should not—repeat, should *not*—look for love in foreign places where the lakes explode.

She was perfect for me.

I was a dead man.

DAVID MCLAURIN

Mortal Sins

Roberto Enriquez is a cavalry officer with every advantage, but compromising relationships, his own personal sense of failure, and the backdrop of a moribund military regime have conspired to trap him in a vicious circle of moral decay. Despite his devotion to duty, Roberto is drawn into a vortex of evil by the blandishments of Colonel Olivarez, the Minister of Security, bringing him face to face with his mortal sin.

'*Mortal Sins* confirms all the promise of this formidably talented young writer's first novel, *The Bishop of San Fernando*. An eerily well-constructed, well-paced thriller, it is sometimes stomach-churningly frightening, sometimes lightly comic.'

A. N. WILSON, *Evening Standard*

David McLaurin was born in Sussex in 1963, a few years after his family moved there from Trinidad, where his father had been in the Colonial Police. He read English at Oxford and has now entered the priesthood. *The Bishop of San Fernando*, his first novel, was runner-up for the 1994 *Sunday Express* Book of the Year Award.

JULY   £5.99   PAPERBACK

Mortal Sins

THE CROWD BELOW the Palace windows that Roberto looked down upon was one of the largest that had gathered there in recent memory, and contained, did he but know it, Nicola Nickleby as well as Strauss and Tanucci.

Strauss had only been aware of the fact that Nicola had bought her ticket for a few hours. The security men employed by Olivarez checked all flight bookings regularly, but because the whole country was in chaos all weekend, thanks to the General's birthday celebrations, it had taken longer than usual for the report to be made. As soon as it had been, Strauss, with Tanucci in tow, had gone to the travel agent and found out where the suspect lived, which was not difficult, since Nicola, in case her flight had to be retimed or cancelled, had left her address with the travel agent. After that it had only been a matter of watching the block of flats and waiting.

It was thought best by Strauss not to arrest the woman at home. Nickleby was dangerous and she had associates. The operation that Strauss had in mind was designed to cause panic in the ranks of her associates; for Strauss resolved that Nickleby should be snatched in the street, and the large crowds everywhere that Saturday seemed to be a God-given opportunity.

It turned out to be easier than he imagined. A woman answering Nickleby's description had come out of the block of flats shortly before two, accompanied by another female. They were followed by Strauss and Tanucci as they made their way on foot towards the Palace Square. Strauss had stood next to Nickleby in the crowd, and sent Tanucci into the Palace to inform their superior officer

203

of what was about to take place – for if anything went wrong, Strauss did not want to be without support. He did not intend to act solely under the authority of a boy Lieutenant. He was resolved to be as well covered as only a man who had once been sentenced to hang could be.

As soon as Tanucci had come back, bearing Enriquez's thoughtless consent, the plan was put into action.

Strauss approached Nickleby amidst the press of bodies, as soon as he could see that her companion was allowing her attention to wander. When he was near enough, he struck. Years of experience with hypodermics meant that Strauss struck cleanly and effectively. The small blonde girl gave a low scream; it was the only sound that she made before fainting under the effect of the tranquilliser.

Isabel's cook was several feet away and craning her neck to see the tanks the better when it happened.

'A young lady has fainted,' she heard someone say.

She turned. She saw a rather brutish-looking man in uniform.

'Clear the way, clear the way,' the man was shouting above the excited noises of the crowd. 'You, Lieutenant, sir, give me a hand.'

A younger man, an officer, was trying to do his best to push through the crowd and come to the rescue. The cook noticed that it was Nicola that they were helping. She caught sight of her pale blonde face for an instant, so noticeable in the crowd. She tried to attract their attention, but in the press – and there were some more tanks appearing now, and the crowd was applauding them deliriously – no one heard her. She tried to force her way towards Nicola, but unluckily the crowd was surging forward at that moment, and no matter how hard she tried, she found herself being carried away in the opposite direction. She screamed, but her scream was drowned by the cheering. Now ever further away, she saw Nicola's lifeless form being carried away to an ambulance, and the two officers getting in it with her. Then the ambulance drove off, sirens blaring, hardly noticed in the midst of the military festivities.

(The ambulance had been General Messina's idea. He knew

women fainted in crowds on hot days. He had wanted people to think that the Junta thought of everything.)

After a few hundred yards, Strauss informed the ambulance driver and the medics that their vehicle was being requisitioned for military purposes. They did not argue. Then Strauss drove to the Army Navigational School, where he left the prisoner under the guard of Tanucci. He then returned the stolen ambulance to its station in Palace Square and decided to report his brave exploit to Captain Enriquez, who he knew would still be inside the Palace.

By lucky chance Strauss found Roberto just as he was coming down the stairs.

'Sir,' he said. 'We've caught her.'

Roberto looked at him coldly, for he was in that moment making his escape. Elena would be waiting for him at her mother's flat, and he had promised to be there in a few minutes. He did not want to be late.

'Oh very well,' he said. 'Don't do anything rash.'

'Will we see you soon, sir?' asked Strauss.

'I expect so,' said Roberto, knowing that it was not true, but hurrying away all the same.

'It is so hot!' exclaimed Isabel de Calatrava a few hours later. 'Do you like my hat?'

'Yes, and yes,' said Maria Enriquez.

Isabel was certainly dressed for the occasion. It was as if an overweight flamingo had settled on the lawn.

'We do seem to keep on meeting, don't we, my dear?' said Isabel. 'Of course, I know why.'

'You do?'

Both ladies were standing under the shade of a pine tree, where they were taking refuge from the broiling sun; it was now six in the evening, but still as hot as ever. They were at the Garden Party, being held in the Marine Gardens to celebrate the General's birthday. In the background a military band was playing excerpts from the operas of Verdi adapted for brass. Little flocks of overdressed people were visibly wilting in the sunshine, uncertain as to why they were there. The Garden Party had been another idea of General Messina's; he had heard of similar things being held in London.

'You see,' explained Isabel. 'Everyone is talking about Captain Enriquez. Your young man is so well thought of. He is quite the handsomest man in the Army; and he is so clever. They say that Colonel Olivarez has noticed him.'

'So you tell me.'

'I am sure of it. But I don't seem to have seen him here anywhere.'

'He hasn't come,' said Maria. 'He told me that he wouldn't come and that no one would notice his absence. He preferred to slip away once the parade was over.'

'So modest of him,' gushed Isabel. 'And also rather clever. Perhaps it is best to keep one's distance at present. Do you think the President will appear?'

'I really don't know,' said Maria. 'I am sure the poor man would rather be left alone to die in peace.'

'Talking of death,' said Isabel, 'there is the Archbishop.'

The Archbishop was standing a little apart, as Archbishops do. Father Morisco stood next to him, like a sentry on guard, very neat, smiling and black. He had just been speaking to Captain Zondadari.

The Archbishop was deeply troubled. He had hoped to see the President. That was why he had come. Instead he had seen General Messina who had given him bland assurances about the Father of the Country's health.

'I am wasting my time,' said the Archbishop quietly to himself.

'Your Grace?' asked Father Morisco solicitously.

'We are all wasting our time,' said His Grace.

'And time,' said Father Morisco, surveying the ladies in hats and the men in their medals and dress uniforms, 'time is running out.'

It was, thought the priest, the swan-song of the régime.

A feeling of doom hung over the Marine Gardens, for the party was having quite the opposite effect to the one General Messina had intended.

'You saw the tanks?' Sir Nigel was asking.

'No,' said the rather dull man next to him, who happened to be the American Ambassador.

'Quite right. Neither did I. They invited me to do so, but I refused. They were trying to prove a point I suspect. They want to show the people that they are still in business – a show of might. I was damned if I was going to be a party to that. They can go down the plug without me. Her Majesty's Government won't be very sorry to see them go, either.'

'My Government,' said the dull man, 'thinks the same as yours.'

'Have I asked you whether you have a helicopter?' asked Sir Nigel, with what he hoped was an air of indifference. (For Sir Nigel had given up hope for his furniture once Isabel de Calatrava had been unable to provide him with an aeroplane, and was now thinking primarily of himself.)

'You have and I do,' said the American; attempting a witticism he added: 'The balloon will soon go up.'

'He's had three strokes already, he can't eat solids any more, and he won't survive the week,' said Sir Nigel.

'I've heard the same,' said the American.

'He will die.'

'He will die,' echoed the American.

'Hernandez will take over,' said Sir Nigel.

'Messina will take over,' said the American. 'But it won't be a peaceful transition.'

'In a country like this,' said Sir Nigel with a rare flash of insight, 'things have been peaceful for far too long.'

*   *   *

Some twenty miles away, in the very hunting lodge that his father had caught his death of cold in, Roberto said: 'Caballero is dead.'

Elena had been talking about him, on and off, all afternoon. He had felt pushed past the limits of endurance. She had used the same phrase over and over again. She had been unable to bear the uncertainty any longer: she said that she had to know whether he was abroad, or in jail or dead. He had not come to the country to hear this, but to escape from it. He felt he had to stop her talking about Caballero. So he had told her.

She heard the words and was silent. She thought of Caballero alive and she tried to picture him dead, but failed.

'How?' she asked.

'The death certificate said that he was killed while attempting to escape from protective custody,' said Roberto shortly. (This was true.)

'Oh,' said Elena, numbed by the realisation that her very worst fears were now confirmed.

'I didn't know whether to tell you or not,' he said at last. 'But I supposed only the truth would put your mind at rest. There is something else that you ought to know as well; I think you ought to go abroad. They say there is going to be a war. The President is almost dead, and when he is finally dead, there will be a fight. I want my mother to go too.'

They were sitting on the terrace as he said these things to her; he kept his eyes on the view as he spoke and did not look at her.

'And you?' she asked, at last.

'I've got to stay here. And if I'm killed that will be that. It is no more than I deserve.'

'Why?'

'Everything has gone too far,' he said mechanically. 'I can't walk away from it now.'

He was thinking of Caballero.

'I won't leave the country unless you come too,' she said.

'Heroism doesn't mean anything any more. It's all false. If only you knew.'

'But knew what?' she asked.

'It is over between us,' he said. 'The only thing you can do for me now is to go away.'

'What?' she asked.

'I don't think we should meet any more,' he said lamely.

'But I want to know why not,' said Elena. 'Look at me and tell me why. What has happened? If you don't tell me why, I'll never leave you but hang onto you like a harpy.'

'I don't want you to hate me,' he said.

'Oh God, you are so vain,' said Elena in exasperation. 'You are so damned vain. You want to be so perfect, and you want me to go away because you can't bear the thought that I might realise that you are less than perfect. You expect me to be there whenever you want me, and now you expect the opposite. You think that you are so important.'

'Then why don't you leave me?' he said, looking at her now.

'I wish to God I could,' she replied.

He reached for his packet of cigarettes and lit one.

'You never used to smoke,' she said reproachfully.

'There are many things I've never done that I do now,' he said.

'There's one thing you've never done, certainly,' she said bitterly.

'Well go and find someone who will,' he said cruelly. 'I don't want you. I don't think I have ever wanted you really. It has been bad enough having my mother hanging over me all these years; but I don't want you making me into a hero as well. Don't you realise what I have just told you? Can't you see what has happened? I killed Caballero. I did it myself. I shot him in the back of the head, and I did it because I hated the man for what he had told me about myself. I am a murderer. Now leave me.'

Elena looked away and wept.

'How could you?' she asked.

'It was very simple.'

'But why?'

'You will never know, because I will never tell you.' Then he added: 'I lost my temper, but that isn't an excuse. I lost my temper because he told me that I was a sadist and that I couldn't ever love a woman properly, at least not you. At least that is what I think he said. I can't remember. It all seems so strange. Killing him was so easy, and I have never killed anyone before now; in fact I can hardly use a gun.'

He laughed uneasily and a little hysterically, amazed at the stupidity of it all.

'I never thought it possible that you could be violent or cruel,' she said, trying to understand him. 'You've always been so shy and reserved and frigid.'

'But I am not,' he said viciously. 'You've never known me.'

She got up and went into the house. Roberto was left to watch the sunset on his own. He knew he had done the right thing. He had told her the truth. He was a murderer and he was beyond her forever because of what he had done. He was cut off from the rest of humanity, just like the first murderer who had borne the mark of Cain. As he sat on the terrace realisation of the solitude of his existence swept over him. He was condemned to live among people he had no liking for, and he was separated forever from those who might have given him comfort. He thought of his long dead father, and of his disapproval; and he thought of his mother, who had brought him up as a hero's son, and was angry. She would condemn him, but she had made him what he was, because she had never told him that there were other things higher than the call of military duty.

But this last thing was not true; he was unjust to his mother, just as he was unjust to Elena. He was the way he was because he was still the boy who blushed, the boy who could never bear to be proved wrong about anything. And he could not admit that he was wrong now. He could not turn back: only a miracle could do that, and he did not believe in miracles any more.

He wondered where Elena was, and wondered how he could face her. He felt a glow in his cheeks. Behind him lapped the swimming-pool; and because he could not go into the house and

210

confront her – for he had murdered her friend – he decided he would go for a swim instead to escape the heat and to eradicate the traces of guilt on his face.

From within the house Elena heard the splash of him diving into the pool. Her tears had dried now. Caballero was dead, and she felt that she too had played a part in his death. Caballero was dead, but even that could not break the bond that existed between her and Roberto. She could not and would not let him go. She was stubborn, and she loved him with all the stubbornness of love. So she took a towel from the bedroom, combed her hair and went down to the pool edge. There he was furiously doing his lengths, and eventually he noticed her shadow on the water and stopped. He took the towel from her, and getting out of the water used it to cover his shoulders. She noticed that he had gone for his swim still wearing those particularly hideous knee-length shorts that the military always wore under their trousers. He sat down by the edge of the pool, dripping and silent, and reached for his pack of cigarettes.

'I can get dressed and drive you home,' he said, lighting one.

'No.'

'Then I can get someone to come and pick you up, if the telephone is working.'

'No,' she repeated. 'I've decided that I've got to stay here with you.'

'You may wish you hadn't,' he said.

'If I do, I promise that I'll never tell you,' she said. 'Caballero isn't important to me any more,' she added with an effort. 'But you are. And whatever Caballero said to you, isn't true. I – I believe in you.'

'Because you love me?' he asked.

'Yes.'

He contemplated his bare feet and wondered if love could redeem him after all. How odd it was to think that he had shot Caballero, and yet here he was, sitting in his shorts by the side of the swimming-pool, smoking a cigarette, with her next to him.

He had broken all the rules. He was in a state of mortal sin, as he had killed another man; he was now a lapsed Catholic, something he had never been before. All his previous life seemed to have disappeared, but he felt no different. He had crossed some barrier, and found himself on the other side, and yet that other side was not the desolate terrain that he felt it ought to be. She still loved him; she would not leave him; and the thought of that almost made him angry once more.

He put his arm around her, as he had been in the habit of doing in the five years he had known her. He felt her warmth against him, and he wondered if he should continue to hold out against her any longer. Had there been any virtue in his long self-control? Could he not, at long last, be what she wanted? It could not make any difference to the state of his soul, after all. All that was finished. He had killed Caballero, and in the process he had killed his own soul.

Darkness fell.

Later, Elena watched the distant lights of the City, and knew that amidst the indifferent mass of humanity that composed it, lay Caballero's body. The clothes he had worn on that last day she had seen him, his watch, and the ring he always wore, perhaps these would be returned one day to his next of kin neatly wrapped in plastic, accompanied by some impersonal death certificate. Until then, Caballero had a tenuous existence in a sort of suspended animation. Until then he would be disappeared, not dead. Only he was dead, and Roberto had killed him. But she was forgetting that already, and felt a small residue of guilt for it, a guilt that concerned only herself. She had not realised how little Caballero had meant to her in comparison to Roberto. But this had always been the case. All those afternoons of conversation she had had with Caballero had been about Roberto. She had never really been interested in Caballero himself, only interested in him as an interlocutor for conversations about Roberto. And those conversations had cost him his life; her indiscretions had killed him. She was sure of that. And if Roberto had not killed Caballero he would not have made love to her either. One mortal sin led to another. That was equally sure.

Behind her Roberto lay asleep; she could hear the calm regular sound of his breathing in the darkness. He was very beautiful as he lay there. She wondered if she were pregnant; it was quite possible; in some ways she would rather like to be pregnant. It would be the definitive bond between them. The possibility of a child had never occurred before. On the very rare occasions when it might have arisen in the past there had always been enormous self-control on his part which had prevented it. She had never taken the various steps women were supposed to take for the prevention of conception; nor had he done what men were supposed to do; these things had never been necessary. Up to now there had been some invisible barrier between them; but this evening something had changed.

The barrier had dissolved between them. They now both knew each other. He had killed Caballero, and she was an accessory after the event. She had joined him in his crime, because she could not bear the thought of him being apart from her. It was as if she had given him that most precious thing of all, her soul. Perhaps she should have done as he had suggested and left him, but it was too late for that now, and she was bound to him forever.

Something that sounded like a bomb went off in the distance. He awoke with a start. She stayed at her window and heard him pad over to her on silent feet. He put his arm around her and she felt his warmth behind her. His chin nuzzled against her shoulder and she took his hand. His proximity comforted her and drove away the slight sense of melancholy that she was beginning to feel.

'They are letting off fireworks from a ship in the bay,' he remarked. 'Twenty miles away.'

'Don't tell me that it is a clear night and that we have a wonderful view,' she said.

'Why not? It's true,' he said. He was not used to having his conversational opening challenged in this way. 'Are you feeling sad?' he asked her.

'Only a little. Are you?'

'Not particularly,' he said, knowing that this was not true. Melancholy had taken hold of him. Caballero was dead; there was a strange intimacy between himself and the murdered man, and now there was this new intimacy between himself and Elena. The way he had let Caballero see him had meant that he had been unable to hide from her any more as well. His isolation had been breached, and the days of his self-sufficiency were over. He was feeling sad. He had failed to be the complete man of duty.

'I'll resign my commission,' he said. 'Do you want me to?'

'Very much,' she said.

'There will be a war soon. I don't want to be part of it. I can't be,' he said, already feeling the hold she now had over him. He wondered if she was pregnant already, but did not know how he could frame the question without sounding as if he were already trying to squirm out of his responsibilities.

'You have gone all red,' she remarked, putting a hand on his cheek and holding it there, studying his face in the reflected light of the fireworks. 'Again,' she added, for he had been like that as he had made love to her.

He looked at her and began to long for his clothes and a cigarette – it was uncomfortable this way she had of looking at him and seeing into his soul. She knew his secret.

'Marry me,' he said, reaching for his pack of cigarettes.